MORE THAN A GAME

Jerome D. Gibson

More Than A Game

Copyright © 2010 by Jerome D. Gibson

ISBN 13: 978-0-9814645-1-0
Author: Jerome D. Gibson
Cover/Back/Interior Design/Graphics:
David Greenway: xray4u2@hotmail.com
Editing: Kimberly Figgs: figsie@yahoo.com
Models: Steven and Latricia Miles (Couple):as5828@wayne.edu
          Daniel Reyna:dreyna623@gmail.com

Calandra Publishing books may be ordered through booksellers or by contacting:

Calandra Publishing
P.O. Box 1296
Lincoln Park, MI 48146
www.keepingcash.com
1-313-355-7774

Printed in the United States of America.

Dedications

This book is dedicated to God, Jesus, my beautiful wife Calandra, my mother, Carolyn, my father, Duranda, my older brother, Duran, my sister, Cynthia, my brother, Derek, my Grandparents, my nephews and nieces, as well as the rest of my family. I have to make a special dedication to Margaret Ogletree and my students at DSA who helped inspire me to write this book. To Nathan Tate, thanks. Brother David Greenway, Sister Kimberly Figgs, Latricia Miles, Steven Miles, and Daniel Reyna I can't put into words what your contributions have meant to this publication. Mrs. Beeman, Mr. Lunsford, and all my teachers who gave me their best, now I can do the same by giving my best.

I also want to THANK YOU for purchasing my book. Without your support this project would not last.

5

A preacher once said, "Life comes down to a few choices that will either improve or destroy your life, so choose wisely." I chose to allow my anger to lead to the choice I am making today. My arm was stretched toward my one-time best friend, who was frightened because my gun was an extension of my arm as I pointed it at him. He pleaded for his life, but I wasn't hearing it. As I looked in his eyes, I felt my finger squeeze the trigger tighter and tighter before I heard a gun go off. I saw the bullets enter his flesh. When his body hit the ground, I heard his last breath as everyone around me laughed and celebrated. I was numb at the sight of the blood flowing freely from his lifeless body. Everything happened so fast, but there was only one thought on my mind…

2

"Game!" I shouted when Los and I beat everybody on the court that day. We were in a zone, just knocking them off. One after another, they fell under the onslaught of Los and me. It got so bad that some of them gave up and quit before the game even ended. It helped that Los and I were unbeatable ever since we were 14 years old, only ones we couldn't always beat were grown men. Playing three hours straight didn't faze us because we knew that in a few days, we would be starting our senior year and summer vacation would be over. It felt good to play game after game, which allowed me to take my mind off things even for a little while. Our last game was against Ant and his boy Trey, two drug dealers who were the neighborhood weed men. They had been selling so long they didn't know what a real job was. As we continued to beat them, all they kept talking about was how much money we could make if we worked for them.

"Y'all could easily make $200 a day working for me." Ant said.

"It's easy money, more than what y'all would make working at Mickey D's." said Trey.

Their words were tempting, but I wasn't trying to hear it because I already had a lot on my mind. But Los, I noticed, was really listening to them. He always talked about making money and being the man one day. He would have gotten into the game long ago if I hadn't been in his ear talking him out of it. As we beat them yet again, Trey started talking.

"Ant, it ain't no use talking to them, not with church boy over there. He believes that being broke makes him a good Christian; yeah, it's just a waste of time."

Trey always came at me like that. I had to handle that fool last summer and he never got over it. Every chance he got he took a shot at me; like when he talked about how he could beat me in 21, how I had no skills, and that Los was carrying me. So, I played that fool like I never played before. Everybody from the hood was watching so I had to gain my respect. Mission accomplished as I beat him in a 16 to 4 shut out; and everybody in the hood knows that if you have less than 6 points when someone scores 16 on you, you've been shut down and humiliated. The spectators laughed him off the court, and it took a while before he showed his face there again, but business dictated that he couldn't stay away too long.

Finally, I spoke up.

"Like I said before, I'm not interested."

"I guess y'all gone be broke all y'all life," Ant replied.

At that moment, they said they had to go and left Los and me alone on the court.

"Did you hear that? $200 a day! Do you know what we could do with all that money?" Los asked.

"Yeah, I hear you, but you know I can't do that, it would break my momma's heart and I can't deal with that right now." I paused. "And you know how much she's into the church." I said.

"I know but that's still a lot of money." He hesitated as he asked. "But how is she?"

"Not now, I just don't want to talk about that right now." I sighed and looked down at my watch. "I got to go."

"Alright man, catch you later." said Los, as I walked away.

I darted home and as I walked in the door, I saw my dad's face. It was moist and his eyes were red from crying. I asked,

"What's wrong?"

I waited with baited breath, knowing, but not wanting to acknowledge in my heart what I already knew he was going to tell me. He caught his breath and said,

"Your mom...She, she's dead, she died..."

Dead! Dead! That's all I heard as my dad told me my mother was dead. Although I knew in my heart, I still couldn't wrap my mind around those words. I couldn't allow them to sink in and become so real and so final. When the paramedics came, they used the paddles on her trying to revive her. I could only stand and watch as her lifeless body jerked back and forth. I couldn't help thinking about how much I needed her, so I cried out to God.

"Not now. God, not now!"

Tears flowed down my face when the paramedics stopped trying to revive her. I felt empty and heavyhearted. I kept thinking about how I tried to do what she, the preacher, and everyone in that Church told me to do. They told me to pray and I prayed. I prayed; begged, bargained, and made promises that if God saved my mother I would do anything he wanted. I just really wanted, no, needed him to save her. I couldn't see how I could go on without her. She was my whole world. Dead, how could this be? She was so faithful to God, she believed everything the preacher said and everything in that book she was always reading. I went along with what she said and did because we were so close. I loved her with all my heart and now she was gone. The agony I felt was unbearable. My body went numb as it hit me that everything she'd taught me seemed to be one big lie. What was the point of believing and trusting in God? When I really needed him, he played me. My mom is dead, and I began to think my friend Marcellos, or Los as we called him, is the only one who ever told me the truth about God. Los always said,

"He is never there when you need him."

At that moment, they put my mom on the gurney and covered her face as they carried her out of the house. I ran outside and looked as they loaded her in the back of the ambulance. I couldn't help myself as they begin to drive away I hollered;

"Momma! Please, Momma!"

In that instant, I made up my mind that I could never believe God or a preacher again.

"Let me help you with that."

My dad said as he saw me struggle to get my tie on. As he went through the motions of helping me, I was still in disbelief that instead of getting ready to start my senior year, I was getting ready for my mother's funeral. All week I really didn't say much to anybody. So many people came over to our house talking about how much they would miss my mother. They talked about all the things she did for them and how they were sad to hear that she had passed. My older brother Keith, who was in the military for the past four years, was able to get leave from the Army to come to the funeral, but he was going to meet us at the church because his flight would get in too late to meet us at the house. My older sister Endia came over this past week to help make the arrangements with my dad. She tried her best to talk to me because she knew I was hurting. Endia knew how close I was to our mother and that this was killing me inside. Endia and Keith were a little older than I was, Keith was 23, Endia 21, and I was 17, so by me being the youngest, mom's death hit me the hardest. I just kept looking in the direction of my mom's bedroom, hoping she would walk out even though I knew she was gone. My thoughts were interrupted by my dad saying,

"The limo is here. It's time to go."

My dad couldn't pay for the limousine so he used my mother's credit card to rent the limousine for the funeral. I knew that was wrong, but if he hadn't used it we would have had to ride in his broke down car. None of us was having that. Not today. We wanted to arrive in style to send my mother off. The ride to the church seemed so long even though it was only 20 minutes. Keith was waiting for us at the funeral home in his Army uniform. When he saw Endia, he hugged her, then me, and finally my dad. He started crying because he was not here when our mother died. He kept saying,

"I should have been here. I should have been here."

We were instructed to line up by twos to proceed into the Church. When we walked in, everyone was standing as the preacher, Elder Murphy, recited Psalms 23,

"The Lord is my shepherd; I shall not want. He maketh me to lie down in green pastures: he leadeth me beside the still waters. He restoreth my soul: he leadeth me in the paths of righteousness for his name's sake. Yea, though I walk through the valley of the shadow of death, I will fear no evil: for thou art with me; thy rod and thy staff they comfort me. Thou preparest a table before me in the presence of mine enemies: thou anointest my head with oil; my cup runneth over. Surely goodness and mercy shall follow me all the days of my life: and I will dwell in the house of the Lord for ever."

As Elder Murphy finished and walked to the pulpit. We walked up to the casket and I watched as my dad look at my mom. He stood there and stared. For the first time I saw the hurt that he was feeling from losing my mom. Until this moment, I never would have thought about how much my dad was hurting, he knew and loved my mom longer than all of us and still would have loved her even after we formed our own separate families. My dad stood motionless, it seemed like he was not going to leave from looking at my mom in the casket until Endia went up beside him, whispered in his ear, then walked him to his seat. When Keith saw our mom lying in the casket he couldn't stop crying. He looked, paused, and then turned to go to his seat. He just kept rocking back and forth blowing air and talking to himself. The ushers provided him with tissue to wipe the tears off his face.

When I walked up to the casket, everything became slow and quiet as I stood over my mom's lifeless body. Tears began to build up and then flow down my face. I knew she was dead. I was there when they tried and couldn't revive her; however, coming face to face with her in her casket thrust me into a new emotional reality that my mother was truly gone. So many thoughts began to run through my head as I kept thinking how I would give anything to hear her voice or feel her touch again. Knowing I would never hear her say "My Little Davie" again wiped me out. I thought Endia would have to come get me too, but I received strength from somewhere that enabled me to lean over and kiss my mother gently on her cold cheek. My last words to her as I leaned and whispered in her ear were,

"I love you, mommy."

I took one last look at her as I went to my seat.

After we all sat down, there were many people who walked by, said a few words, and hugged us, some I hadn't seen in a long time. Under normal circumstances, I would have been happy to see most of them, but my attention was focused on the fact that my mother was gone. I kept bracing myself for when the casket would be closed because I didn't want to lose it, and then Elder Murphy got up and made an announcement,

"By request of the family, the casket will remain open for the duration of the services."

I immediately looked at Endia and she looked back and smiled. I knew she was the one who convinced my dad to do this. I truly appreciated my older sister for caring for me like this. She knew I couldn't take seeing the casket closed on my mother. After the Elder sat down, many people gave reTreys about my mother. I have to admit; knowing she touched so many lives actually gave me some comfort. I watched in disbelief as a familiar looking man walked up to my mother's casket and bid her farewell. Many people whispered as he walked by. I later found out he was the drunken bum my mom would give money and out of respect for her he showed up sober. That's just the type of effect my mom had on people.

Many thoughts ran through my head as the eulogy was given. I started feeling a little anger build up in me because he kept talking about how merciful God is and how my mother trusted in that mercy until the end. In my mind I said,

"Merciful. If God was so merciful, why are we sitting here right now? My mom would still be alive."

Thoughts like this kept coming to my mind, being triggered by the ongoing message about how good God supposedly is. However, after the funeral was over and we recessed, the only thing on my mind was how the rest of my life will be without my mother. My thoughts were interrupted as Keith said,

"The funeral director said for us to get in the limousine, so we can go to the cemetery."

We all piled into the limousine, including Keith, to go to the cemetery. When we arrived, we gathered at the mausoleum as Elder Murphy opened with,

"Ashes to ashes, dust to dust...."

Hearing these words brought new meaning to me. Even though I heard this saying many times before, I came to realize how fragile human life is. My mom and I used to talk about how when I graduated high school we would all go to Red Lobster and I could order anything I wanted from the menu. We talked whimsically about me, her son, the college student. All that planning and talking was just a pipe dream. Now here we are, at her funeral. We planned and hoped for a future that would never happen. What a waste of time.

After we left the cemetery and rode back to the house, I saw my dad crying. It shocked me because I saw two sides to him, the man who stood motionless at my mom's casket and the one who used to argue a lot with her, nothing physical, just words. Endia gave him some napkins as she put her arm around him and told him,

"Daddy, remember mom loved you very much and you know her love will be with you always."

He looked up, wiped his face and said,

"I know, but I need her. I've always needed her. She put up with me, even when other women would have left. I can't stop feeling like a part of me has died inside."

Endia kept talking and holding dad. It took him a little bit, but he got himself together because he knew everyone was waiting for us at the house and he was not about to go in there like this. When we arrived, right before going in, my dad signed a receipt to pay for the limousine. We entered the house and everyone approached us saying how glad they were that we were home. I paid this little attention as I looked at the couch my mom used to sit on being occupied by a woman and her kids. That brought back to my mind the last conversation we had,

"David, you are a chosen vessel for God and don't you ever forget it. If you ever stray, remember the Prodigal Son and don't let pride get in your way." She said while coughing.

At the time, I was feeding her soup because she was too weak to feed herself and couldn't hold anything else down.

"Promise me!" she insisted as she grabbed my arm.

"I promise." I said as she lay back down.

"Boy, we really are going to miss your mother."

I emerged from my thoughts and turned to see the face of my no good uncle, whom we hadn't seen in three years; not since the day my dad threw him out of our house because some money came up missing. Of course, he didn't know what happened to it. He kept talking about how close he and my mother was and how he should have been there when she passed. I couldn't take it anymore, I kept thinking,

"Is he for real?" So, I responded sarcastically,

"You're going to miss her. You haven't come around or called in years!"

He glared at me with disbelief. He couldn't believe I called him out like that, but he knew he was no good; everybody knew, and today I was not going to deal with his hypocrisy.

"We haven't seen you in three years, since you stole that money. You act like we all of a sudden got amnesia and forgot what you did." I said in anger.

All he could do was stare as I walked away from him. My anger was getting the best of me and talking to him was not helping.

I continued to think about my mother in that casket and it made me remember that fateful day five years ago that changed everything.

It was late and my mother was coming home from work. My dad always told my mom that he didn't want her to work that late, but we needed the money. With three kids and a husband who hardly made any money, what was she supposed to do, let us starve? She stepped off the bus and as she was walking home, she was attacked and raped. The cops were no help. They said they would check into it, but we never found out who assaulted her. It took many months of therapy, and even through all the pain and suffering, she stayed faithful to her Church. She still prayed to God and never blamed him for anything; even after she found out, she was infected with the AIDS virus. All I kept hearing from everyone at her Church was that God could do anything and that he would heal her of this disease. They had prayer line after prayer line, anointed her with oil, and held mass prayer, but nothing worked. Her condition continued to get worse as the days went on. Each of us was affected differently from what happened to our mother. Keith went and joined the military to get away from this dreary situation. Endia stayed until she turned 18 and moved. She did come by quite often, but she felt she couldn't stay because of her deteriorating relationship with my dad.

As the youngest, I was the hardest hit by this tragic turn in our lives. I was closest to my mom, and it was extremely difficult and painful to watch, as this healthy, energetic woman became a frail, bedridden skeleton of her former self. But, she always told me to pray. It was as if she was obsessed with making me pray and get as much of God's Word in me as possible. Of all my siblings, I was the only one she made go to Church. My dad didn't care one way or the other, seeing he was not a Churchgoer himself, but he didn't stop my mom from making me go. She tried to get Keith and Endia to go, but because they were older, my dad would tell my mom to let them decide if they wanted to go. And of course, they never did, but still my mom always maintained that it was me that needed to go because of what she felt God had in store for me.

"David, God has something special for you. I know you don't understand now but one day he will show you. Just remember, if you're ever in trouble call to him and he will hear you. Don't let pride get in your way."

I tried what she said, I called him, asked him to save her, but he didn't and she's gone, another victim of AIDS and rape, a statistic. And she won't see me graduate, I thought as I stood at her funeral. At that moment, Los came up and hugged me. I knew he understood because his mother died when he was only three years old. I looked in his face and saw that he had been crying and for the first time I realized that Marcellos was feeling the pain of losing her, too. My mom would always do little sweet things for Los, like making him cookies and little cakes. It got to the point one time that I asked her to stop doing these things for him because she was my mother. But, she would tell me,

"David, what I do for him is nothing compared to what I do for you. Wouldn't you like it if someone took the time to show you the love you would have gotten from me had I died?"

I felt so bad after that conversation; I never said anything like that again, I was just being selfish. Coming back to my senses, I noticed Los began to speak,

"Your mother showed me love and I am going to miss her."

"Yeah, that's how she was."

"You know if you need anything, I'm here."

"Yeah, I responded, and thanks."

"A thousand dollars?!"

I exclaimed as Los showed me the money he'd made in just five days selling marijuana. Four months after my mother died, Los and I hadn't really hung out much. He was never home and he always seemed like he was too busy to kick it. I did notice that Los started to hang out with Ant and Trey. So, it didn't take much to put two and two together. Today for some odd reason Los told me he had something to show me after school. I knew something was up with Los because his gear was much better now than ever. Los used to wear everything nobody wanted, but in these last few weeks, he had clothes that only a drug dealer could afford. I waited for him at the old court where we used to hoop, until they built the new court we play at now. I have to admit, I never imagined he wanted to see me to show his roll of $20 bills. Los begin to speak,

"Yeah, and this is just the start. This is a lot of money, and it's still a lot out there." He continued to smile.

The thought hit me about how much money he made in five days as compared to my dad's two-week check for $500. My friend was making a lot more than my dad, working for Ant and Trey.

"Los, man, who do you, sell to, to get all that money?" I asked in amazement while looking at the wad of cash still in his hand.

"What are you, the Feds?" He grinned and then continued. "I mainly sell in the high school. Ant and Trey are too old to be hanging around and selling in school, so they got me to do it. Man, it's so easy that I'm basically finished before the end of the day."

In my head, my thoughts tripped over themselves as I contemplated what I could do with all that money. Shoot, it was Christmas season and $1000 would buy a lot of gifts. My dad already let me know that Christmas had to be postponed until he got enough money. He had been saying that for years and nothing had changed. At our house, since my mother was raped,

Christmas never happened. Years ago, Endia was fed up with all of Dad's broken promises and this was one of reasons why she moved out. I couldn't blame her for leaving because out of all of us she was the one who was hurt the most because she believed in a man who couldn't deliver. For a brief moment, as I eyed the money still in my friend's hand, I thought about snatching it and running, but all I could do was grin.

"Man, what you gonna do with all that money?" I asked in anticipation, hoping he would kick me a few dollars.

"Jordan's, here I come. You know I got tired of wearing those Payless shoes and now I don't have to deal with those Goodfellow boxes anymore. Now, I can make everybody shut up and take notice. With money and gear, the girls won't know what hit'em."

He grinned and I couldn't blame him. Los grew up on hand-me-downs from my family and goodwill specials. But, what was really sad was everyone knew it and would clown him every chance they got. Things were especially bad for him when we returned to school after Christmas break and everyone had new clothes and all he had was the tight clothes from the Goodfellows box. I couldn't imagine living life like Los was forced to, mom dead when he was three and a broke drug-addicted father who barely fed him. Los often grew tired of people talking about him, so he had lots of fights. He had so many fights I thought he would be a millionaire if he was a professional boxer. His thought was,

"I may not be able to stop them from talking about me, but I can win the fight."

Seeing how happy he was, I realized he was going to sell drugs to gain respect and to get the things he really wanted.

"David, I'm telling you, this money is good and easy to make." He paused. "You know we can make this money real easy. Teachers and kids are buying weed from me. There are so many buying every day I can't keep up with them. Man, I went shopping the other day and when I dropped the cash on the counter, they were running like roaches trying to get everything I wanted." He said with a grin.

"Man, I don't know. The money looks good, but you know my mom was always against me getting involved with all this stuff. She really believed that God would be displeased." I said.

"What do you believe?" Los asked.

Quickly I said,

"I guess I believe the same as my mom."

What? Where did that come from? I couldn't believe I'd just said that because the day my mother died, I said I didn't care about God or no religion. Los said,

"Well, what about your dad, how does he feel about it?"

"I don't know, I replied, occasionally my dad smoked a joint, which really upset mom, so I really don't know."

At this time, I was a little confused and it showed on my face and could be heard in my voice. Los took advantage, and knowing him, I knew this conversational turn was leading up to something.

"Look, we're friends, like brothers right?" Los asked.

"Yeah." I said. "We been boys since first grade."

I nodded as I wondered where he was going with this.

"So, just listen when I say this and I am not trying to be mean. You know how I've always felt about God and this religious stuff. So, think about this, your dad who smokes and is not into the Church like your mom, is still alive. But your mom, who believed in God, is not. If there was a God, don't you think it would be different? I mean wouldn't God have protected your mom that night when she was attacked so she could be here instead of your dad?"

I felt the anger build up in me. It had been a long time since I'd wanted to clock Los, and had anybody else said what he just did it would've been a done deal speaking about my mom like that. As much as I hated to admit it, he had a good point. I thought about all those days she went to Church, prayed, gave money and time to God and it got her nothing but dead. Then a thought came to me. Why should I continue to live off my dad's lousy money when I could make four times what he's making? These thoughts kept running through my head, but still, I had to think about it, so I said,

"Los let me get back to you on that."

"Alright. I'll catch you later, but you know I'm not going to wait forever." Los sounded disappointed as he walked away.

On the way home, I continued to think of what I could do with all that money. I felt the coldness of the snow seaping through my old worn out shoes. The cold winter air kept smacking me in my face. I knew I needed a coat and some boots, but with all the money my dad spent for the funeral, we barely had money to eat much less to spend on clothes and boots for the winter. I hated living like this. I've known tough times before, but somehow my mother made those times bearable. I knew my dad was trying his best, but I also knew trying doesn't always cut it. At any rate, I knew whatever decision I made would affect not only me, but everyone around me, and definitely, it would impact my friendship with Los. If I sold with him, we probably would grow tighter because we would definitely have to watch each other's back. But if I didn't, how could I justify hanging with a dealer? Besides, with his new money would he bother hanging with me? My mind engaged in a tormented tug of war over what would make me happy as opposed to what would make my mom happy. I thought of all that money coming in and being able to do whatever I wanted with it. That's hard to pass up. Also, I thought, if I sell I would be turning my back on my mother and everything she stood for, everything she had instilled in me.

I had to stop this mental battle. I had to make a decision. I knew whatever I decided someone was going to lose out. So, squashing the wrestling match within, I decided,

"If anything else bad happens to me today, I am going to do what I have to do."

My thoughts were interrupted when I saw yellow flashing lights in front of my house. I knew what that meant; *the Repo*

Man. As I ran across the street, I saw him hooking my dad's car up to his truck while the neighbors looked on. My dad pleaded with the man. His words, resonating loudly in my ears, reminded me how bad we'd had it these last few months.

"Please, don't do this! You know my wife just died, and I'm still paying for her funeral!" In desperation he asked, "How can I pay y'all back if I can't get to work?!"

The tow truck driver had nerves of steel; he didn't even flinch as he finished hooking the car to his truck and drove away. I looked at my dad and thought,

"So, this is how God takes care of the family of a woman who was faithful to him."

At that moment, I knew life ain't spitting no freebies. No matter how much you are hurting, people only look out for themselves and now it's time for me to do the same.

"You know I'm good for it."

Mr. Smith, my English teacher, said to me trying to get me to give him some free weed. I didn't even flinch; he knew I didn't get down with giving out freebies.

"Alright, how about this, if you let me get by this time, I'll give you an A on your next exam."

I looked in Mr. Smith's eyes as he continued to make this pitiful attempt to get free weed from me. I started to think about how two months had passed since I started selling. Los took me to see Ant and Trey shortly after that repo man incident. Los was happy and talked about all we could do with the money we would be making and how we would have each other's back. Even though Los was happy that I wanted to be down, Trey tried to clown me by saying,

"So, the little church boy wants to make some money." He snickered and said. "Get this fool out of here, he ain't serious."

Los got angry and said,

"Look, what did I tell you. If my boy say he ready, then he ready. Trey, you not gone treat my boy like he weak."

"What you gone do about it?" Trey said with a stern look on his face.

Los began to square up with Trey and I thought it was about to go down until Ant said;

"Y'all calm down." He paused. "David, all I want to know is are you serious or are you doing this cause your boy talked you into it?"

I put what Trey said out of mind because the only thought I had was, "When do I get paid?"

So I said,

"Yeah, I'm ready."

"Alright, my man Los here will make sure that you know how we operate. All you have to do is do what he tells you and you can make this easy money." Ant said.

"Yeah, it's so easy that even a church boy like you can't mess it up." Trey said while laughing.

I got a little agitated at Trey always taking a pot shot at me so I said,

"Just remember this church boy dogged you on the court, so whenever you're ready, let me know and I'll gladly humiliate you again."

Trey stopped laughing and Los started laughing at Trey, as he looked like he wanted to kill me. But, I wasn't worried about him. All my attention was focused on getting paid. Ant began to speak,

"Look, I don't want y'all talking like this. This is business and all this stupid back and forth is bad for it. All of you work for me now, so all that petty arguing stops here or out the door you go."

We all settled down as Ant told Los to take it slow with me on how to sell and who to sell to. Los took me under his wing and showed me everything I needed to know. He showed me how to bag and price the weed. Los would let me watch up close how he sold and talked to the customers. He also let me know how to deal with those who used to buy weed from the competition; this guy name Mike. Los was starting to get all of Mike's customers because Los sold a high quality weed whereas Mike sold weed that looked like it was grown in the backyard. But, Los would get the occasional customer that would say,

"Los, you know Mike's bags are $2 less than yours, so why should I pay more." Ron said

"Yeah, Ron you right, Mike's stuff does cost less than mine, but you know I got the best stuff around, that's why I charge a little more than everybody else. Remember, you're paying for quality, not quantity."

Ron looked and then pulled out his $40 and paid Los for his bag of weed and then left. At the end of the day Los sold all his stash and said,

"You see, Dave. I sold everything between classes and at lunch. You have to be sure that you don't cause undue suspicion or you will get caught." He paused. "Now, today, I made $800, of that $200 goes to me and $600 goes to Ant. As long as Ant gets his $600 he doesn't care how much I sell it for."

I was taking mental notes on how to do this. It took a little bit to catch on, but because we sold in school, it didn't take long. Pretty soon, I no longer needed Los watching over me and I was able to get and maintain my own clientele. Mike, who sold inferior product, was quickly out of business when I started selling. But, there was no love lost. Mike started selling crack, so he didn't really care that Los and I took over selling weed at the school.

Which brings me back to Mr. Smith; I continued to look into his eyes thinking back to how much I used to respect him until he started buying from me. Here he is, college educated, with a full time job, and still constantly coming up short, he was worse than the kids. So, he needed to bribe me with fixing my grades in order to get his fix of weed for the week. A lot of times, I didn't mind because all he wanted was a $40 bag and that meant I didn't have to study for his class. English was the only class I needed in order to graduate. It was never my thing because of my dyslexia. It was hard to keep up with all that Shakespeare and research papers I had to write. I could have gone the Special Ed route, but there was no way I was going to get clowned for being with the slow kids. So, for me it was just dumb luck that selling weed got my English grade taken care of. Also, I promised my mom that I would graduate high school. So, I said,

"Make it the next two tests and we got a deal."

I watched his face drop because it looked like for a brief moment he was having second thoughts, but then reality hit him. There was no one else who would give him a $40 bag of weed for a grade. Mike was done with selling weed and Los didn't care about grades; all he cared about was making bread, so Mr. Smith knew if he wanted the weed, I was it.

"Alright, but you better not let anyone know." He said in a low voice.

"You think I want everybody in my business?" I said as I handed him the bag and started on my way home.

Just about every week this was our routine. I purposely put a $40 bag to the side because I knew he would be asking for it. On my way home I started thinking about the crazy things I've seen since Los turned me on to making this bread. Teachers, counselors, coaches, athletes, nerds, you name it and I bet you they were all my customers. Selling didn't bother me because on the street, weed is looked at the same way cigarettes are; no big deal. Since I wasn't selling crack or some heavier drug, I figured a little weed never hurt anybody. It was funny how a little extra money and gear, had girls at school working so hard now to get it on with me. I mean, these girls never paid any attention to me before, so why should I hook up with them now? I wasn't dumb enough to think they liked me, but no doubt they loved me all the way down to my wallet. However, Los was eating up all the attention, bragging how these girls were crazy about him and not his money. I kept trying to tell him that they only wanted his money and if someone else came along, they would leave him in a heartbeat. He didn't listen, but hey, that's on him.

My dad found out about my "extracurricular" activity because he always kept his ear to the street. He questioned me about who I was selling for and when I told him Ant and Trey, he eased up on me. He knew that the only thing they dealt in was weed and since he considered that, a light drug he didn't say too much. On occasion, he hit me up for a $40 bag and since I was dropping him $200 a week everything was very smooth. I know a lot of people would judge his actions for willingly allowing his high school-aged son to sell weed, but these people were not in our house when the heat was cut off, when his car was repo'd, or on the Christmases, we didn't get anything. Yeah, it's easy to sit back and say he should have did this or that, but unless you coming with some loot you can keep your opinion to yourself. I was enjoying the money, but sometimes I felt a little guilty about selling and letting down my mother.

I was amazed at how much I was selling and how much I was making. As I said earlier, Los showed me how to sell and who to sell to. Initially everything I learned, I learned from Los, but I started doing my own thing when I truly realized as long as I gave Ant and Trey what they expected, I could sell my product anyway I wanted to. Los made a little more than me because he was trying to squeeze as much money as he could, while I made sure that I sold mine as fast as possible. I would put a little more in my bags to sell them faster and the customers knew it. Usually, I would be finished selling by 10:30am while Los took all day. Yeah, I only made $100-$150 a day compared to Los' $200 a day, but that was ok I wasn't looking to make this an all day thing. Los enjoyed every aspect of selling, so taking all day didn't bother him, but I just wanted to sell and get outta dodge. I knew that I didn't want to stay in the life, so for me it was strictly business.

Los, on the other hand, would sell to anybody and tried to get as many people as he could to buy from him. Discretion was not his strong point. Once I got my base customers, I only sold to them and their friends. I was never hard-pressed to sell. My people always came to me and brought new customers with them. It became so lucrative, in fact, that I started sending them to Los because I didn't have enough weed. You have to realize that selling in a school, you could only smuggle so much weed in before people would get suspicious. Since I had a limited amount, many of them would try to get to me before I ran out and Los became their back up. Every day during lunch, I would leave and make a drop to Ant and Trey then go back to school. Often they tried to convince me to take more to sell, but I told them I wasn't interested. When Los found out he thought I was crazy, but I had to work my own strategy, that is--*get in, make your money, and don't get greedy*, because it's usually the greedy people that get caught up. Los started to notice that Ant, Trey, and the customers frequently commented on how well I handled my business, so one day he said,

"How did this happen, I was selling before you and they're treating me like I'm the new guy selling. I just don't understand that?"

I just looked and I didn't think much of it, but I should have. Everything in me knew that Los believed that since he introduced me to selling that I always was supposed to be under him. In his eyes, I was beginning to outshine him and this he could not accept.

People in the game, like me and Los, always seemed to spend a lot of the money on clothes, shoes, and whatever else was hot, but as I said before I ain't planning on making this a lifelong career. I did buy a few clothes, and I even bought a little car. Still, I watched how I spent my money and while I was stacking my bread, Los was spending a lot of his money on a car, girls, and clothes. Even though I was making bread, I never forgot the places I used to shop and the owners would give me deals because they knew me. Los always went to the mall and paid top price for everything. He thought paying more made the clothes better, but I didn't care. If I liked it, I bought it.

I got my car through my dad who turned me on to this little car lot he knew about. The owner bought nice cars off crack heads and if you had cash, he sold them real cheap. It was funny how he and dad seemed to be old friends, but I never remember him coming around. They stood there laughing and talking while I checked out the cars. There were a lot of cars on the lot that caught my eye, but one car really stood out. It was a rimmed out and practically brand new looking. It was a 1983 Monte Carlo. I looked at the tinted windows and I was digging it all the way. I knew a car like this would cost me more than the $2000 I wanted to spend, but I had to ask,

"How much you asking for this car?"

My dad and the lot owner stopped talking and walked over to me and the car. The lot owner looked at the car and then turned to me and said,

"How much you got?"

Now had he said this to Los, he would have been told none of his business, but I am a straight up type of guy and it didn't bother me to tell him,

"I got $2000 and that's all I'm spending."

He whispered something in my dad's ear and they both laughed. Then he said,

"Alright, you drive a hard bargain just don't let anybody know that you only paid $2000 for this ride."

I nodded and was a little overjoyed that I got a nice car to drive without paying a lot for it. The car was a little flashy, but not to the point where a person would think, I spent major loot on it. After I paid for the car, my dad and I stopped and got something to eat. While we were at the restaurant, I asked,

"Dad, how did you know the lot owner?"

My dad looked up and said,

"Stay out of grown folks business."

I knew what that meant. He always said that when he didn't want me to know something, so I dropped it. Later that day I saw Los and he was really digging my car. He gave it the once over and started admiring the rims and the sound system. I could tell he was upset that I got a car before he did.

"So you big time now. You got the new car with rims and a sound system, while your boy is walking. You could have told me that you were going to get some wheels."

"You know it wasn't like that. I saw it and I got it. You know how that is. Like when you bought that motorcycle, you didn't tell me about it either."

Los got quiet. Then he jumped in the ride and said,

"Let's see what this baby can do as he turned up the radio."

A few days later Los went out and bought a 1985 Monte Carlo SS from this car lot where everybody knew the owner overcharged. He paid about $4000 for that car. Then he spent another $3000 on the sound system, tinted windows, and some rims. One day Los asked me how much I paid for my car and I told him,

"Mere pennies."

I knew that ticked him off, but I didn't want him asking a lot of questions. If Los learned about my hook-up, he would have messed up my connection by running his mouth. The lot owner didn't like everyone in his business and Los would have brought too much awareness to his activities.

On a different note, I never really had time to think about girls like Los because for so many years I concentrated on my mother. Girls, who were only trying to ride the money train, didn't figure into the equation for me. Los on the other hand couldn't get enough of these girls. All the girls that were once out of reach for him were now accessible and he wanted them all. He spent a lot of money keeping them happy and on his team. As a result, Los thought I always had more money than he did. Often, he asked me how I was able to pay what I owed Ant and Trey, get good grades in school, have a nice car, and stay geared up. I'd simply smile and tell him I had very good customers. I don't know why I never told him how I managed my money. For some reason I just couldn't bring myself to tell him. I used to think selling together would bring us closer, now I could see that it was driving an invisible wedge between us.

Los really started to change. Not only did he dress in expensive clothes, which nobody else could afford, he looked down on people and was extremely cruel. The roles were reversed, as he became the person who talked about and clowned people. He just wouldn't let up. He was driven by revenge and his new status. He was starting to act like he was better than most of the kids at the high school. He had no love for bums or anybody that lived on the street. I remember one time we were out and this man asked for some change. Los dogged him out and told him to get a job. What kind of crap is that? I felt sorry for the man and was about to give him some change when Los knocked the money out my hand and said;

"You need to learn that you don't give freebies to the homeless, they can't do anything for you!"

Enraged, I looked at him and said,

"Don't ever do that again, man. If I decide to throw my money in the air, it ain't your business!" I picked up the money and gave it to the man. I then turned to Los and said,

"Los, you don't understand, everybody has worth, remember not too long ago you was the one everybody looked down on and said wasn't going to be nothing."

The bum thanked me and said,

"God Bless You. Thank-you, you are the first person who ever stood up for me."

"Yeah, a real bleeding heart, just like his mama."

That statement by Los hit me like a ton of bricks. It slapped me hard across the face like the insult it was meant to be. After all the things my mother had done for Los, in my estimation, he had just spit on her grave. I knew then that things had forever changed between us.

For rich people the golf course is where they make many business deals. In the hood, there is the basketball court where just about every dealer hung out. But, unlike on the golf course, while we were hooping and discussing business, we had to watch out for cops who tried to bust us at the drop of a dime. But for the most part, this area was the place where there was an unwritten truce between dealers. All beefs and rivalries were handled out on the court. Los and I came here many times, but not as dealers. It was different being in the thick of things and to hear as each dealer talked about how to make more money. Some were turning others on to customers who wanted product they didn't sell, but the others did. Since me and Los only sold weed, many of the guys on the court made a lot more money than we did. It didn't bother me because I mainly came up here to hoop not really to talk about business. I was selling all I wanted. But, Los wanted to be in on making more money, so he listened intently as they talked about selling. One day at the court, this crack dealer named William told me and Los,

"Try Jackson Street. That's where all the weed heads live."

Even though we knew people at the court would turn you on to making more money we were a little skeptical about what William said. Los didn't want to say anything to Ant and Trey, so I did.

"Yeah, you know William, the guy that drives that beamer. He told me and Los about this street around the way that's supposed to be crawling with weed heads."

"Straight up." Ant said as he paused. "That guy William turned me on before to a couple things, so he knows his stuff. David, Los I want y'all to check it out and let me know what's up."

"Alright, we will and get back to you." I said.

We checked it out and sure enough, it was so many people on that street that wanted some weed it took Ant and Trey weeks to keep up with the demand.

Just like that, the basketball court could increase your cash flow if you listened out. But there was another side of it I tried not to allow myself to get caught up in, *the challenges*. One time Los and Darnell, a crack dealer, got into it because Darnell said Los didn't have any skills. Los got mad and challenged him to a one-on-one game, winner gets $200.

"You sure you can handle that?" Los said to Darnell.

"Boy, I'll hundred dollar and fifty dollar you to death. Let's play."

Darnell had all his boys there and they watched as Los beat Darnell easily because he just wasn't ready for Los. Los was one of the best street players out there and everybody knew it, but there was always the occasional fool who wanted to try him. After Los got the money from Darnell, Los started clowning him talking about how he beat him and got his money.

"I got two hundred reasons why I'm better than you." He said. "Maybe you ought to try something you're good at, like jump rope."

Los laughed and everyone else started laughing too. Even Darnell's boys started laughing. I tried to stop Los from talking trash because even though we chilled with the violence at the basketball court, it was another unwritten rule not to mock anybody, especially if you just took their money, but Los, I guess, thought he was the exception. Darnell got mad and pulled his gun on Los. I froze. I knew Los was done because we never considered packing because we sold at the high school. Darnell then started on Los as he kept his gun pointed at him.

"Now, what you gotta say? Who's winning now, huh? Give me back my money and run your pockets." Darnell said angrily as Los gave him everything he had.

After he emptied his pockets, Darnell smacked Los with the gun.

"Now son, get outta of here, before I really get mad."

Los walked away to the sound of everyone's laughter ringing in his ears, as they made fun of how he got played. Darnell yelled and said,

"Now, I got $200 reasons why I'm better than you."

Everybody continued to laugh as I caught up to Los, he said,

"Man, that ain't gonna happen to me again. From now on I'm always gonna be strapped. People take you for a joke when they know you ain't carrying, but next time they're gonna get a surprise."

I listened to Los who wiped the blood away from his mouth as we walked to my car. I knew that I had to get a gun too, especially since everybody knew Los was my boy. The game was changing rapidly and becoming more dangerous.

8

"Ninety-nine! Ninety-nine! Ninety-nine!" Our excited chant grew louder as we threw up our hats in celebration of our high school graduation. We were happy that we'd finally made it. Most of us knew we were never going to college and this would be our last graduation, so the celebration was intense. We hugged, cried, and said our goodbyes. I took so many pictures with everybody. Everywhere I looked up, all I kept seeing was the flash of a camera. For the first time in my life, I could relate to why celebrities get tired of people taking their pictures. It seemed like I took pictures with everybody that is except Los. Los was not at graduation because he did not make it. He failed a class back in ninth grade that he never made up, so he needed to go to summer school. I was so happy my dad and siblings were there to see me get my diploma. The only person that was missing was my mother.

Thinking about how my mother and I used to always talk about going to Red Lobster, my favorite restaurant, on this day. I had to pull myself together because I didn't want to spoil this day for anyone especially since I am the first in the family to graduate from high school. Keith and Endia both got their GED, so I was the only one with a high school diploma. We kept true to my mother's word and went out to eat and I was anxious to get there. Just thinking about that Admiral's Feast made me want to jump in the ride and make like Mario Andretti.

As we walked in I looked up and everything slowed down. People were talking around me, but I heard nothing. I was aware of only the slightest movement as I focused and became fixated on the most beautiful girl I'd ever seen. Her name was Valencia, I remembered her from back in the day, but I don't remember her being so beautiful. Dressed in black, she looked almost angelic as she laughed and enjoyed dinner with some guy, maybe her boyfriend. I strolled by as we were seated at a table across from her. I made sure to sit where I had a clear view of her. Then I remembered while growing up, Los had it bad for this girl.

He used to talk my ear off about how much he had to have her. As a matter of fact, she was the only girl Los ever got nervous around. Once when we were in middle school, he worked up enough nerve to talk to her. But she told him no because she was not allowed to talk to boys yet. She was one grade ahead of us and came from a strict family. Los kept trying to talk to her, but she let him know it wasn't happening. He was crushed when her family moved that year. But, he quickly got over it when he found himself another girl.

It's been four years and until today, I never really noticed her, because Los liked her. Also, I was too consumed with caring for my sick mother. But now, I couldn't keep my eyes off her and I wondered what brought her back to town. She finally caught me staring at her. I turned my head quickly as I saw her smile out the corner of my eye. I couldn't believe how beautiful she had become. I never realized I was attracted to her because my boy Los liked her so much. Trying to respect our friendship, I chose not to pay any attention to her. I also realized how silly it was that I was feeling guilty, for being attracted to a girl Los tried to talk to when we were only 12. I tried to keep my head turned but I couldn't help staring at her while everyone continued talking around me.

"Whoa wee! Don't let your eyeballs fall out!" My brother Keith exclaimed loudly, much to my embarrassment. "You're looking at her hard!" Keith laughed as he blurted this out.

He was home on leave and even though he was an Army sergeant, he still was a clown. I saw Valencia chuckle and I knew she'd heard him. I was caught off guard and quickly averted my gaze, wishing I could make a swift exit. But, before I could, I felt a hand on my shoulder and then I heard,

"David? David Jenkins, I thought that was you. Do you remember me?"

I looked up at Valencia and saw all her long black hair and that smile. Time stood still for me and it seemed like forever before I found my voice. At last, I managed to say,

"Valencia, how could I forget you?"

Keith was about to say something else, but I jumped in before he could.

"After all we did go to middle school together."

I was almost hypnotized when she smiled at me, showing her perfect white teeth. I fell for her smile. I felt that the only thing I wanted to do was continue to make her smile. Valencia broke me out of my trance when she said,

"David, it's been a little while since I saw you."

She paused and motioned for the guy she was eating with to come over. I felt a hopeless rush run over my body as I braced myself to hear her say,

"This is such and such, my boyfriend."

Even though we were sitting across from her table, it seemed like he took a long time coming over to our table. When he got there, she grabbed his arm and he looked a little surprised, but then she said,

"This is my cousin Dominic who just got into town."

"He's your cousin." I said.

It was more of a statement than a question. And with a grin I realized I might have a chance with her, but I didn't realize how loud and excited I was until Keith pointed it out, again, embarrassing me. I made a mental note to myself to murderlize him later.

"Man, she got you like that?! You all loud and happy that, he's not her boyfriend, hey wait everybody, Little Davie likes her!"

He laughed annoyingly loud as I turned red, or at least I would have if I wasn't so dark. He knew I hated that nickname except when my mother said it. I wanted to crack his head, but Valencia did something I didn't expect. She leaned in and kissed me. She then turned to my brother and said,

"Little Davie has good reason to like me." She smiled and walked back to her table with Dominic.

At that moment, "Little Davie" became my favorite name and I smiled as I looked at my brother who shut up for the first time, effectively silenced. I guess the day turned out to be pretty special after all. Our table was quiet for a second before my dad said,

"Well, this is shaping up to be an interesting graduation celebration." We all laughed as I continued to look at her.

A short time later, she walked over to my table and handed me her number, with a smile she said,

"Little Davie, call me some time."

Scooting my chair back I said, "I'll walk you to the door."

I was not about to let her go without speaking with her privately for a moment. As we walked to the door, I said,

"Um, I uh, I'm glad to see you."

I thought talking to her would be easy but this was so hard for me. I never really talked to a girl like this before. I was so focused on taking care of my mother I never really had time to learn how to talk with girls. I came to appreciate that conversing with the opposite sex took some skill. But, Valencia was not going to let me off that easy.

"That's all you got to say? Boy, you were staring at me like you saw a ghost, or maybe I simply took your breath away."

I'd forgotten how direct and funny she was.

"Yeah, well you know how it is; you look so good, and remember," Smiling, I reminded her, "You kissed me."

I said trying to be cool and not fumble over my words. For a minute, I wished I had Los' finesse. He never was at a loss for words with the ladies, and here I was with this fine girl who's really feeling me, and I don't know how to respond.

"Well, I had to give you a graduation gift." She smiled again, "and the pleasure was all mine."

Her cousin Dominic pulled up and said,

"Val, we got to go. You know I got to get up early in the morning."

"OK. David I got to go, just give me a call and maybe we can go out some time."

She hugged me as she got into her cousin's car then drove away. I stood there for a minute trying to collect myself to avoid Keith's jokes that I knew was coming once I went back to the table.

As I made my way back to the table, my dad had this nostalgic and faraway look on his face. It was a look he sometimes got when he thought of my mother, but this time it was a little different. It was different because he was smiling as he said,

"David, you know that girl Valencia seems to be nice." He sighed softly. "She reminds me of your mother."

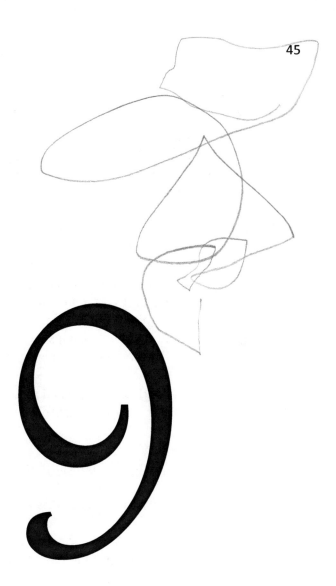

"David, are you nervous?"

Valencia asked with that perfect smile as she tried to calm me down. This was our first date and I was trying my best not to mess this up. It had been a week before I got up the nerve to call her. She sounded so happy to hear from me but she did let me have it.

"So, you found enough time in your busy schedule to call me. Let me get your number before you disappear on me again."

I gave it to her and we talked for about an hour before I asked her out. We agreed to go to the show and decided to take a walk by the marina after we ate. It was a nice night but I didn't really know what to say after we ran out of things to say about the movie. We started holding hands when she said,

"Your hands are all sweaty and you really haven't said much. Are you nervous?"

I looked at her and realized I was used to talking to the fellas, not the ladies. I was still surprised that this beautiful girl wanted to go out with me.

"Yeah, I am." I said.

I was used to being blunt and honest. I figured, why not be straight up?

"To be real, you're my first date, if this is what it is." I said tentatively.

"What? What about the prom?" She said surprised.

"I didn't go to prom. A lot of time has passed since we last saw each other." I said, trying to find the right words. "You were in the eighth grade and I was in the seventh when my mom got sick."

"Yeah, I remember everybody talking about it."

"Well, shortly after that you moved away. During that time, I helped to take care of her, until she died last year. Every day I rushed home to be at her side and tried to nurse her back to health, so I didn't have time for girls or going out."

Valencia spoke with a concerned tone,

"David, I would understand if you don't feel comfortable talking about your mom. I know how close you were to her." She said softly.

I attempted to continue, but decided not to.

"Yeah, look, I know I'm doing badly on this date. We're supposed to be having fun not talking about my mother." I said.

"That's ok." She said. "I like that we can talk about something real. Other guys I've dated were only interested in getting in my pants and never really talked about anything they really cared about."

She grabbed my arm and moved close to me. I will admit I was nervous, but I wanted her close. Every guy knows when that special girl touches you it gives you a feeling you can't begin to describe. This girl had me floating.

As I drove her home and walked her to her door, she paused and bit her lip.

"David, you remember back when your boy Los tried to talk to me in middle school." I nodded. "Well, I wished you would have tried, I always knew that it was something special about you. While everyone else was all into themselves, you were taking care of your mother. That really touched me."

She kissed me again, a kiss that lasted longer than the one in the restaurant. I smiled and said,

"You gone get enough of kissing me off guard."

She smirked and said, "Like you care." She gave a little peck and went into the house.

As I drove home that night, all I thought about was her. I just kept replaying the night in my head. I came up on that bum I'd seen long ago when Los and I had just started out in the life. He sported the usual sign '**WILL WORK FOR FOOD**'. I don't know why, but I stopped and gave him $100, maybe I was just happy from being with Valencia. He was surprised and happy when he saw it was $100 and said,

"Youngblood! Thank you and God bless you. If there is anything you need from me let me know." He coughed. "I don't know why you are so nice to me, but I do appreciate it. Remember Youngblood, *Proverbs 19:17, "He that hath pity on the poor lendeth unto the Lord; and that which he hath given will he pay again."*

"That's alright. I know everybody sometimes needs a helping hand."

Then I drove off. I guess I was tripping. My mother used to say that all the time and now I was hearing it from him. I found out later that he used to be a preacher, but got caught stealing money from the church.

As I walked through the door, my father said with a smile,

"So you went out with girlie from Red Lobster."

I nodded. My dad looked at me and I could tell he was trying to think what to say to me, when he finally said,

"Does she know that you sell?"

It was an awkward silence in the room as I stood in disbelief that he said that. I asked,

"Why you ask me that? This was only our first date."

"David, if this girl is anything like your mom and you think she is special, you need to be up front with her." He paused. "If she finds out from somebody other than you, you might lose her."

I tried to downplay my involvement,

"Dad it ain't like that, this was just our first date I don't know how this will even turn out."

"You just don't realize, but I…" Dad stopped himself and said, "David just remember what I said, it's better to come clean and deal with it, then to let it come out and create drama and trust issues that you can't overcome."

I knew he was right but I couldn't let on that I was feeling what he was saying because it felt weird talking to him about this. When my mom was alive she was the one I talked with, my dad was always working. I dropped the conversation, went to my room, and went to sleep.

Valencia and I kept seeing each other. I just couldn't wait to talk with her and be around her. In the back of my mind, I sometimes wondered what I was going to say to Los about going out with her. I know a lot of guys would say I was wrong for going out with Valencia, but I didn't see anything wrong with it. Besides, I didn't have a lot of girls, this was my first one and I wasn't about to give her up just because of some middle school crush that Los had. That's crazy. Besides, he had lots of girls and he would never have a chance with her anyway, so that settled it for me.

We were out walking one night. The moon was shining bright and clear. As I looked into her pretty brown eyes, she blessed me with that smile, which made me calm and nervous all at the same time. Valencia looked at me and said,

"David, I really like being with you." She sighed. "I mean I feel so close to you, like there are no secrets between us." She stopped and looked at me. "You opened yourself up to me and I know that was hard for you, but I promise you I will always be careful with your heart."

As she held my hand, I felt I was betraying her in a way. My dad's cautionary words reverberated in my head; I knew I needed to tell her about my selling weed before anybody else did. If I didn't she would feel that I'd lied to her. I had been talking to her about my mom and all the trials that my family had gone through in caring for her, but I never mentioned that I was selling weed for Ant and Trey. I knew when I told her she would be very disappointed. I knew her feelings for me might change. For the first time since my mother died, I couldn't bear the thought of hurting or letting down someone, I cared about. I already bore the guilt of having turned my back on all that my mother had taught me. And I knew Valencia must have heard things since we sold at school, but she probably just brushed it off. Finally, I couldn't contain myself. I had to come clean with Valencia; I knew this could end our relationship but I owed it to her to be honest and upfront. I don't know why, but it mattered to me how she saw me.

"Valencia, I have to tell you something." I looked into her eyes with deep remorse as I continued. "I feel the same way about you." I bit my lip. "Valencia, I want everything to be right between us because you are the only girl I have ever had feelings for. Every day since we started going out I can't wait to see or hear from you. I'll admit you make me feel like I did when my mother was alive. I don't ever want to do anything to hurt you or cause you to be disappointed in me. I know it's weird, but with you I feel complete."

I looked her straight in the eyes and everything in me screamed, '*Don't tell her, you're going to mess things up!*' I blocked out the voice and proceeded.

"There is something about me you don't know and I have to be the one to tell you." I sighed. "I have been selling weed at the high school for the past few months."

She looked at me like she couldn't believe what was coming out my mouth. Her expression crushed me, but I continued.

"After my mom died, my dad's car got repo'd, and he struggled to make ends meet. He struggled to pay off my mom's funeral expenses. I tried convincing myself that I was doing it for him, but I started liking the money I was getting."

"So, you like being a dealer?" She asked as she gently pulled her hand from mine.

"No, I'm not saying that. I like the money, not the job. Valencia, I started selling long before we saw each other again. All I sell is weed, nothing else."

"So that makes it right, David? I really like you and all, but I can't be with a drug dealer. Yeah, I know weed is not crack, but it's still drugs. Eventually, you are going to want to make more money. When you do, that will mean selling harder drugs which could put my life in danger."

Valencia gave me that look that every guy hates to see come across his girl's face, so I said,

"Valencia, that won't happen. Weed is all I'll ever sell. If I become stupid enough to sell something that will endanger your life, then leave me."

Valencia paused, looked at me, and then she put her hands in mine and said,

"David, I appreciate your being honest with me, and I want to believe you, but I need something from you too." I looked at her with anticipation as she continued. "I need you to swear on your mother's grave that you will always be honest with me and let me make up my own mind if I can or want to continue in this relationship."

I looked at her. She wanted me to swear on the grave of the woman that I loved more than my own life. I didn't like this, but it made sense. She knew if I swore on my mother's grave there was no way I would ever go back on my word. I read somewhere once that a man's word is his honor. Looking her in the eyes with honesty and trepidation, I said,

"I swear."

Then she hugged me as we continued to walk. I'd almost lost someone special to me because I was dealing. That day I made a vow to never put myself in a situation that would cause me to risk losing someone I really cared about.

10

The day came when I had no choice, but to talk to Los about me and Valencia. We had been going out for about two months now, and this time we both drove and met up at the show because she had some things to do afterwards. I kissed her goodnight and as she drove off, I heard;

"Why you kissing my woman? You played me! I thought we were better than that?" Los shouted when he saw Valencia leave.

Los and I weren't hanging much with him in school during the summer; he had that 9th grade class to complete for graduation. So, while he was in class all day, I was hanging with Valencia. It was weird though, Ant pushed Los to finish high school because he said it would be important later. Ant even paid for him to go, which if you knew how cheap and stingy Ant was you would be as amazed as I was. I tried to explain to him that we never got around to talking about me and Valencia because he was always busy, either in school or selling everything else he couldn't at the school.

"I was going to holla at you about us, but you were always busy with school and all." I said.

"I thought you was my boy. You know you never talk to anyone your boy likes or talks to." Los said.

"Come on, that was middle school and you know her parents wouldn't let anybody talk to her." I said trying to calm things down."

"I hear that, but you still were supposed to give me first crack at her since she came back."

"And I was supposed to do that why? Because of your middle school crush?"

It was like we were two dogs and Valencia was the bone. This was weird for me because we were both, in a way, competing for a girl. But then I said,

"And I know you ain't talking, with all the girls you got. You're still mad about the one that got away. You can't have them all, so man, get over it already. And anyway, where would you fit her in, what, as girl number 12?" I said in disbelief.

"Yeah, alright, but still you know if it wasn't for her parents, she would be with big money Los, not little money Dave."

He said in a malicious tone as he tried to laugh it off, but I knew that Los was not feeling me talking to Valencia. He was truly resentful, but he had to get over it because I was not about to give her up.

"Yeah man, only in your dreams." I said as I left.

It was the last day of summer school. Los had just completed his last class to graduate. He called me the night before telling me that Ant and Trey wanted to see us. After hanging up the phone, I began to wonder why they wanted to see us. Sales this summer were not as good as the regular school year, so I wondered if that was it. But, surely, that couldn't be the reason because Jackson St. more than made up for the losses from the school. I still managed to sell all my stuff on Jackson St. I hated working the street scene though. I was so used to selling at the school in a controlled environment and getting outta dodge, but working on the street, you were totally exposed and didn't know what to expect. I had no choice since I was not in summer school and it would have looked suspicious if I was hanging at the school everyday. Los joined me later in the day because he couldn't sell all he had at the school. As I arrived for the meeting with Ant and Trey, Los was already there. Immediately they started talking to us about how we couldn't sell at the school anymore since we'd graduated. He felt it would draw too much attention if we continued to sell at the high school. Los wasn't going to let this goldmine go without a fight. So, he questioned Ant,

"Why, we still know people, so why not?" Los asked looking upset.

Ant went on to say that, we would bring too much attention to ourselves because we had no legitimate reason to be there every day. I could understand that, but Los wasn't hearing it.

"Man you got to give us something. You can't cut us off like that; we've sold a lot for you. I know things were not as good at the school this summer but you know when school starts back and with Jackson St. we'll be on and popping."

I knew Los really liked the bread, but I never thought that he would resort to begging to work. But I guess the money had a hold on him and nothing was going to stop him from making that bread.

"Look, I know how much y'all sold for me; you don't have to remind me." Ant said sternly. "I have to admit that this summer, is the most I've ever made at the high school and Jackson St. put me over the top. But, remember, I've been doing this for a long time and I don't need you telling me how to run my business." He paused. "Now, as I was saying, my next move for y'all is to set y'all up with something else. I can't let my two best runners go, now can I."

I felt a little odd about this. Ant sounded like he owned us by calling us his runners and taking credit for the sales we made this summer, but I listened to him anyway.

"David, you said you're going to the community college up the way, right?"

I nodded.

"So, since Los is finished with high school now he can enroll too." He paused again. "I want y'all to start selling on campus. I've been trying to break in there for a while, but people can look at me and tell I don't belong on a college campus. Think about it, a lot of your former customers from the high school are going there, too and you can maintain the old, and in the process get new customers."

I could tell this idea appealed to Los because I saw the look on his face as understanding dawned, he could make a lot more money. Our high school only had 1000 students whereas this community college was 4000 strong. But, I really never thought about selling at the college because in my mind I always separated what I did in high school from what I would be doing in college. The thought of making more money appealed to me greatly. But I knew Valencia would be on campus too, and I was concerned that she would have a problem with me working the campus. Just thinking about the look on her face when I told her I was selling weed overwhelmed me with guilt. She didn't like it, but she knew it was only weed and nobody got killed for selling weed. Also, I never took product around her and she never saw me handle my business. But, to let her know I would be selling on campus might rub her the wrong way.

"I don't know, it is one thing to sell at the high school, but on a college campus? They have armed security guards, and working security cameras. Besides, how do we know we won't make a mistake and sell to a cop?" I asked.

They laughed. Trey said,

"It's not like we're running a high scale drug cartel, we're just selling a little, and if you get caught all the cops will do is take the drugs from you unless you're carrying a lot of weight."

Trey continued, "Otherwise you won't get any time for selling weed."

He was always rationalizing things. He was more or less Ant's right hand and the brains behind their operation.

"David, think about it, the most y'all made was $200 a day, but at this college y'all could easily make $500 a day."

Los' eyes lit up. He was calculating all that money in his head. I hurried up and said something before Los did.

"That means we'll be carrying around a lot more weed, making us easy targets."

"David, you got to leave high school behind, man, this is college, where you pick your own classes and schedule. You can choose to take classes in the morning, afternoon, or night. So you can take your usual amount and sell that. Then do your drop, get some more, go back and sell that, then drop again. Get the picture? You won't be carrying any more than before."

I thought about it and it sounded reasonable. There was no more risk involved, I simply needed a little more time to sell and I could earn even more. It sounded simple, but as I learned in this life, nothing is ever as simple as it seems.

To keep my promise, I told Valencia about me selling at the college. I knew she didn't like it, and she reminded me not to bring it around her. When we registered for classes, I made sure that my classes started an hour after her because I figured I would sell during that time, so I wouldn't run the risk of exposing her to my business. The money was coming in like crazy. I never realized that so many college students and professors smoked weed. I knew a few did, but there were so many people that wanted to buy that I had to increase my selling time to four times a day. It was as if they couldn't get enough. Mr. Smith, my high school English teacher, turned me on to a few of his friends who were professors at the college; of course, he did this for two free $40 bags. Then my regulars from the high school turned me on to a few upper classmen on campus. With all these customers, I couldn't believe the money I was making. It's one thing to think you are going to make a certain amount, but to hold that amount and even more, it was unreal. I made $700 a day, sometimes more. It was obvious Ant and Trey never guessed that the college would be this profitable. They didn't count on the fact that college students had jobs and not just money they got from their parents. And all the parties, especially the frat parties, brought us some major loot.

Los was making a lot too, but he always tried to make more. He became the victim of his own greed. His attitude was *"The more you make, the more you need to make and the more you have to spend."* He was always saying,

"The real money is in sitting back like Ant and Trey and having people work for you."

I knew Ant and Trey made a lot more than us, but I didn't care, because $700 in one day was more than my father made in 2 weeks. Los on the other hand started building his own crew on the side. Once Ant and Trey saw their profits quadruple at the college, they gave up the high school and that is when Los moved in. He recruited a few of the underclassmen at the high school, turned them on to our old customers, and paid them $100 a day. Ant and Trey didn't care because Los had to get his supply from them anyway, so they continued to make money from the high school regardless of having let it go. One day, I think it finally clicked with Los that the money was in supplying not selling. He said,

"Think about it, we are the ones taking all the risks hustling to sell while they sit back and wait for us to bring them the money. Now, if we were able to get their connect, we could make and keep all the money for ourselves."

I looked at him and could tell that he was planning something. When Los made his mind up about something he usually tried to think of a way to make it happen. He said,

"I need to find out who Ant and Trey is buying from so they can supply us. If I could buy directly from their connect I know I can start making the real money." He paused. He looked at me with this funny look like he was about to tell me something big. He said,

"The only way I'm going to get to this connect is to get close to Ant."

"That would happen only if Trey was out the picture and you know he ain't going nowhere." I said.

"You right, but you never know, things happen."

I looked at him and knew where he was going. Trey either would get out of his way or be moved out of way. Since that day Los got punked on the basketball court he had a 'take no prisoners' attitude. Los got himself a 9mm. It was only a matter of days after he got his gun, when he took Darnell out. He never admitted it, but when Darnell's body was found, he had 9mm slugs in him. I asked Los if he'd done it. He just smiled and said,

"You never know."

Then he snickered and gave me a look that answered my question.

I knew something was up because Los always had everything mapped out before he made a move or said anything. I think he was trying to feel me out to see if I was down with his unspoken plan. When he was about to make a major move he always wanted to bounce it off me as if he needed my approval.

"You know the only way Trey will be moved out of the way is in a body bag or jail."

"Yeah, I know." Los said as he drifted once again into thought.

"And you know that if he wound up in a body bag, Ant would be on the lookout for whoever did that to his boy. And as far as jail, Trey doesn't do really anything to go to jail, so it's going to be tough to get him."

I said trying to talk Los out of this without directly saying it. But, Los said,

"All it takes is just one mistake and who knows, but you're right he would be tough to get rid of."

This conversation became more uncomfortable for me. I wanted to ask Los what he was thinking, but on the flip side, I didn't because knowing him I was afraid to know what was in his mind. After talking with Los I walked away thinking about our conversation. Los knew he didn't have to worry about me snitching because I didn't care for Trey anyway and Los was still my boy. So, I wondered if Trey would wind up like Darnell. This was all crazy to me that Los, my boy since 1st grade, was contemplating killing Trey to get access to the connect. I guess I could have understood if Los wasn't making any money, but he was making quite a bit. Then I remembered my mother telling me,

"….the eyes of man are never satisfied." Proverbs 27:20.

Meaning no matter how much he gets, he always wants more.

13

Ant and Trey were like night and day. They were like the flip sides of a coin and complemented each other well. They both started selling when they were 14 and now they were 23 years old. Trey was Ant's sidekick because Ant had the suppliers and was the one who fronted the money. Ant was a business man. If he owned a legit company, he would've been the next rising star in corporate America. He knew how to capitalize on a good idea, regardless of where it came from. All he cared about was making more money. He was not afraid to mix it up with whomever if necessary. But, he was not overly confident, he knew there was the potential for trouble from dirty cops, not because he was selling drugs, but he was making real good money and one day they'd want their share. So, Ant cut a deal with a lot of the cops. After all, why have the irritation when you can have more freedom by spreading a little money? Ant was direct about what he wanted and an effective decision maker, but he was not as prone to handling the details of the business. This is where Trey came in.

Trey wasn't your typical dealer. He mainly kept to himself, but was always thinking about ways to make money for Ant and himself. Trey was more detail oriented. He was the one who convinced Ant to sell weed instead of crack because selling weed was easy money with little to no competition or danger. He realized that selling weed would allow them to make money in places that were easier to access then the harder drugs. Selling weed in the high school would be no problem because weed is looked on by most people like cigarettes and alcohol, a problem but no big deal. Also, his premise was that everyone was on the lookout for crack dealers and the deadly competition among them, so weed sellers fell far under the legal radar. No doubt they made less money, but still there was enough that they could be satisfied. They were always loyal to each other. Also, Trey was not a user he always kept his head clear. So, for Los to get this guy he really needed something good.

14

"What did you say?" I asked Los over the loud music at the club. It was summer, and our first year in college was complete. We decided to go clubbing. We made a few contacts, but we were there really just to enjoy ourselves. Growing up Los and I always wanted to hang at the club because we thought it was the place to be. But, to be frank, now that I was here I wasn't impressed. I thought there was more to club than what it was. I found out quickly that everything in the club revolved around money. Guys gave it out and women found ways to get as much of it from them as possible. The first night me and Los got into the club, we asked this woman where the bathrooms were, and for some reason she thought we wanted to talk to her so she replied bluntly,

"Until you buy me a drink, we have nothing to talk about."

We looked at each other and then laughed because she thought that was our pick up line. I know she felt like a fool when she found out we truly wanted directions to the bathroom and nothing else.

Los was really digging this place, though. He couldn't get enough of the money and the women. Even though we were technically too young to be in the club, Los felt at home especially with the women. He always liked older women even when we were growing up, so this was like heaven to him. Don't get me wrong Los was not going to give up the girls our age, but he still liked his older women too. And in the club there were all types; drug addicts, prostitutes, doctors, lawyers, teachers, social workers, you name it they were there trying to hustle. Los wasted no time; he hooked up with a corrupt social worker who turned him on to getting some free food stamps. Getting and using food stamps didn't bother Los because he always would say,

"Why spend my money on food when I could use those food stamps for it?"

Los was really making the club work for him, I mean hey this is the life he wanted and I could dig it, but I just wasn't into this scene. It was too crowded and filled with too many backstabbing fake people. I mean one week a guy is with one girl then next week he's with her friend and vice versa. I just couldn't deal with the double-dealing and backbiting. The club was also a place a dude could get caught up with the worst thing to cross his path while trying to get his hustle on: *jailbait*.

The club was full of underage fully developed girls who thought this was the place to be. Being overly developed, no one questioned their age. It was harder for a guy to get into clubs because there was no money in a guy looking older than he actually was. The owners depended on the number of pretty women who came and as a byproduct, brought the crowds and the money with them. Therefore, these young, older looking girls were a money pot and many club owners looked the other way, if the girl was banging. You really couldn't be mad at them because the equation was simple: banging girls equal hustling guys plus money. The owners really got into promoting the fact that they would have pretty women in their club. Promotions like Ladies Night, Ladies Half Off, etc., are all a ploy to get hustling guys to come in and drop them dollars. The guys would buy women drinks and spend even more money to impress them. The prettier the women, the more money they spent. So, in most of the owners' mind, if it takes an underage girl to make this happen, then so be it.

But, with all these young fine girls in the club, there were a lot of guys who got caught up fooling with them. I would hear a lot of guys who said that getting caught up with jailbait wouldn't happen to them. Yeah right. I found it laughable to hear these guys say how they can spot a young girl as soon as she opens her mouth; as if they are really interested in what she has to say. However, I know that no matter how smart, strong, or intelligent you are, one mistake can change everything. Trey learned this lesson in the worst way and became one of those guys who got caught up. He had a baby on the way by this girl named Tina. She wasn't from around here, but from the other side of town and like so many others she liked to hang at the club. Most clubs had an age restriction. Patrons had to be 21 or you had to know somebody on the sneak tip. It cost me and Los a few bags of weed to be allowed into the club. But like I said if you were a female like Tina, standing six feet tall with a banging body and Pocahontas looks, hey, getting in the club was not a problem. When Trey saw Tina, he was on her like a heat stroke in the middle of summer. Dude was trippin as he pushed past me and Los because he knew he had to make his move. He knew if Los saw her first, it was over. Next to Los, Trey wasn't what you would call a girl's first choice. Trey couldn't help himself. He wanted her from day one. Trey bought her drinks and stayed by her side all night until she agreed to let him take her home. As time went on, Trey kept saying he liked her because she was quiet and always let him take the lead. He said with a woman like that you knew she wouldn't tell anybody about your business, so to him she was a keeper. He hooked up with her before he knew she was jailbait because he had no doubt that Tina was older. She always hung with him late at night and stayed with him over night. Tina's food stamp getting parents were always gone or high. So, when Trey would pick her up they never said anything as long as she brought home some of the money he gave her.

Trey discovered Tina was well under aged one night at the club, when Los, Valencia, Los' Social Worker girlfriend, Kelly, and me were all at the club. Kelly saw one of her coworkers and went over to talk with her. After she left, Trey and Tina came over and we all started talking. I introduced Valencia to them. As they spoke with each other, out of the corner of my eye, I noticed Kelly and her coworker looking in our direction with a shocked expression. I nudged Los and whispered,

"Check out your girl and her coworker looking and pointing, I think something's up."

Los cut a quick look and agreed. Kelly later motioned for Los to come over to her and she whispered in Los' ear. Los came back over to where we were standing and said,

"Trey and David, I need to talk to you alone." Los said with a self-satisfied smirk on his face.

I told Valencia I would be back and we walked outside the club and Los began to talk.

"Trey." He paused. "You know my girl Kelly works at the FIA office across town." Trey nodded and Los continued.

"The woman she's with is one of her coworkers. It turns out that Tina, along with her parents are her clients."

Trey and I looked at Los and then at each other, waiting for him to be clear. So, Trey said,

"So what you saying?" He said a little irritated. Trey was not one who liked to be kept in suspense.

"Man, that girl Tina is only 14 years old."

Silence fell. I looked at Los then at Trey, I noticed Trey had this stone look on his face, which quickly turned to anger. He shook his head and said,

"Ain't no way that girl could be no 14 years old!"

"I'm telling you she ain't legal, Kelly's coworker Cynthia is the caseworker for Tina's parents."

Trey paused and was about to say something, but then in a rage ran back into the club. Next thing I know I see him coming out the club dragging Tina behind him. He practically threw her into his car and drove her home. Valencia later told me that she was talking with Tina when Trey came into the club, grabbed Tina's arm and yelled,

"You 14!!"

Tina looked scared as she tried to say something, but Trey continued to rant and rave,

"I said are you 14!? You need to speak up with a quickness!" Trey said angrily.

He looked at her and Tina said nothing, so he said,

"You mean to tell me that my woman is only 14?!" He said loudly.

He spoke so loudly in fact, the music seemed rather soft by comparison, as everybody around him started looking and whispering to each other. Trey looked as if he could kill her as he glared angrily at her. Then he threw his hands up and walked away. At last, Tina said,

"Trey, don't be like that, I'm sorry!"

Trey looked at her and said,

"I want you to hear this very clear, *little girl,* as far as I'm concerned you're dead to me, you don't exist."

Silence fell between them and I guess Tina got mad and said,

"You can't do this to me."

She tried to grab his arm, Trey pulled away. Then she shouted,

"Trey, I'm pregnant!"

He looked up, and his deadpan expression was unreadable. Then he grabbed her arm, and dragged her out of the club to his car.

Such revealing news was all people could talk about. I mean, people just couldn't believe how young Tina was. Nobody directly kidded Trey about the Tina incident because we all thought she was older, so we kind of understood how he got caught up. What was really messed up was finding out how young she was and that she was pregnant, all in the same night. A few days later, I heard he gave her money to get an abortion, but she didn't go through with it. Trey didn't want to have a kid especially with a 14-year-old girl. He was upset, but tried to play it cool by throwing money her way and keeping his distance. He thought he could do what he normally did when things got tough for him; he tried to throw money at the problem. But this was the mother of his child and he was soon to learn that you can't treat your baby's mama like you do all the others.

Los and a lot of the other guys thought the situation was funny, that Trey was having a baby by a 14 year old. But, I thought what he was going through was sad. I couldn't imagine how I'd feel if I'd learned that my woman was in fact, a 14 year old child and pregnant. I don't know but being around them kinda made me uneasy by how cold hearted, they were towards Trey. I mean there was no love between me and Trey, but I still wouldn't make fun of a guy when he is down like this. I just thought that was plain wicked and cruel. But, I do remember what my mother used to say when you are dealing with wicked people that don't fear God,

"You have to watch out because as Proverbs 12:10 says …the tender mercies of the wicked are cruel."

In the back of my mind, I know Trey probably would have laughed at them if the shoe was on the other foot, but still I know he was jacked up over this situation.

15

"David, wake up!! Wake up!"

My dad said as he shook me. I opened my eyes startled as I looked up at my dad's face, which had a horrified look on it.

"Did you hear?! Did You Hear?!" He sounded frantic.

It was late morning, and I was waking up from being out all night with Valencia. We had celebrated our last night before a new semester of classes began, so I was tired. It was strange, my dad never got off work this early, but he was home now. I knew something had to be up so I quickly asked,

"What's wrong?!"

"They hit us! They attacked America! They crashed planes in New York. They ran planes into the World Trade Center!"

I was still a little grougy from waking up and I couldn't understand what he was saying.

"They crashed planes into what?!" I said confused.

Instead of answering me, he quickly turned on the TV and we watched the planes as they hit those towers over and over again as the news continued to replay the tape. I was in disbelief and couldn't think of anything to say, I just sat there unable to move. My dad's face had no expression, but I could see the intense fear in him. The only other time I remember him having this look was when he went to Church and it seemed like the preacher was talking about him. He always blamed my mom for putting all his business in the street.

"I don't know why you always telling those preachers all my business, trying to put me on front like that."

"Leroy, you know I don't tell anyone about the things you do, you need to pay attention because that is God warning you to get yourself together." My mom said.

"Yeah right, the only way they knew about this is because you have loose lips."

My dad would always rationalize things away in order to justify what he thought was a reasonable explanation. This time though he just didn't have an answer or a clue as to what to make of the planes crashing into the World Trade Center, and I could clearly tell that this shook him. What I saw on the television was a couple of hours after the first broadcast, which was why my dad's job sent everybody home early. I looked at my dad as he looked like he was in a trance and then suddenly he snapped out of it and said;

"I'll be right back."

I sat there looking as my dad left my room thinking about what all this meant. I heard in history class about Pearl Harbor, but nothing like this. I wondered was this it for America and what would become of all of us. I thought of Keith, who was in the military, and instantly asked God to protect him and all the soldiers. For an instant, I was surprised that I prayed to God even though I turned my back on him. I couldn't shake the fact that I was worried about Endia, I just didn't know what to do. Then I thought of Valencia and grabbed the telephone to call her, I wanted to make sure she was okay. She was at home and a bit shook up by what happened, so I kept talking with her trying to comfort her.

"It's going to be alright, baby. Don't worry about it, I'm here for you."

Our conversation just went on like this for a few minutes before I began to hear crying in the background and told Valencia to hold on. The muffled sound had come from my father's room and as I walked in, I saw him on his knees praying. I felt the wind knocked out of me as I heard my father say,

"God, forgive me, my wife told me that I needed you and I didn't listen. I know that I did not come to you when she was alive, but after today Jesus I want you to be the Lord of my Life."

I was shocked and bewildered by what I was hearing. I didn't know what to think. Here was my dad, the man who fought my mom every chance he got when she even mentioned Church, God, or Jesus; now he was praying and wanting Jesus to be in his life. He was crying and praying because of his fear of some planes that had crashed into the World Trade Center? Seeing him like this was too much for me. I mean you were denying God all this time, but when you get in a tight, now you want to pray. He was the biggest hypocrite, only calling on God when he got scared. Completely repulsed, I turned and walked back to my room.

The college was closed for the next two days, so I spent most of my time with Valencia watching every report about the attacks. Keith managed to get in contact with us to let us know he was ok, which was a huge relief. Also, Endia called and came over and I was thankful that not only were my dad and siblings ok, Valencia was also. Unfortunately, there were so many families that were not able to say this. I saw so many names of the people who were killed in the terrorist attacks flash across the television screen, it made the whole situation surreal. It amazed me how many people thought this was the end of the world. I didn't hear much from Ant, Trey, or Los for that matter because things had slowed down a lot after the tragedy. It was hard to get product or move it, because everybody was on high alert, so we had to chill anyway.

Valencia and I watched TV to see if there were any new developments. We began to talk about how short life is and how so many people died in that disaster.

"David, looking at this really makes you think about how important it is to treasure those dear to you. You just never know what might happen." She paused. "I know all those people didn't wake up thinking they were going to die as a victim of terrorism."

"Yeah, you're right. I mean I couldn't have imagined being in that plane looking as we got closer and closer to those buildings and then realizing the plan was to crash into them. Man, what a way to go." I said in pity and disbelief.

Valencia hugged me and I held her. At that split second we looked at each other and I said,

"If you were in one of those planes," I shook my head. "I don't know what I would have done. It scares me to think of losing you." I paused and looked her right in her eyes and said.

"Valencia, I love you and I want to always be with you."

She looked at me with a surprised look because this was my first time telling her I loved her. She quickly said,

"David, I love you too. I don't know what I would have done if you were in one of those planes either. There is so much I want out of this life and I know that when this blows over I will be more determined than ever to fulfill my dreams."

At that moment, I just held her and sat quietly for a long time. I'll admit the intimacy I felt towards her at that moment as we shared in each other's vulnerable moments left me speechless. Everything seemed so insignificant while we held each other. The money and drugs were not important, knowing that my life could be taken just like that. Thinking about death and the decisions I have made, led me to believe that if I wanted to have a future with Valencia I knew my days as a dealer were numbered.

I left Valencia's thinking deeply about what we talked about. I kept thinking about how everything between us had changed tonight when I told her I loved her. I felt we were no longer just dating or even boyfriend and girlfriend, but something much deeper. I have come to realize that love is weird because it's hard to explain, however, you know it when it happens. I don't know what it was, but I just knew how I felt about her.

When I walked into the living room, I saw my dad sitting in his old chair smiling. He hadn't smiled like that since before my mom was raped. The thought crossed my mind that he could be high, but I asked,

"Dad is everything ok?"

He smiled and said,

"Never better son." He paused. "You know, your mom was right."

He looked so peaceful as he continued to smile. This was the first time I can remember that he looked happy without being high. I don't know, but something was different about him and I intended to find out what.

"She was right about what?"

I said in disbelief because I knew their relationship was always filled with bickering, when she said the sky was blue he said it was green, you know what I mean?

"Tonight, I went to your mother's church and got baptized in Jesus name and filled with that tongue talking Holy Ghost." He paused. "I'm saved and she was right, this is the best thing to ever happen to me."

I listened and couldn't believe what he said. This guy, who'd refused to step in a church while my mother was alive, was now wrapped up in the middle of some religious epiphany and going to church—my mom's church. He says he is saved and God has accepted him, a fair and just God. Yeah, right, I thought as he continued,

"The only regret I have is that I should have listened to her sooner." He paused."Son, I know you were upset when your mom passed, I was too, but you still need God."

I listened as he tried to get me to come to Church with him telling me I needed to change my life. Hilarious! Here he is, in church less than a minute trying to tell me what I needed.

"Is this a joke?" I asked with anger building inside of me.

"David." He hesitated, "There are a lot of things that must change in order for my house to be pleasing to God. From now on, I can't have you selling weed anymore while living here. I can't continue to support you selling drugs and knowing it's wrong."

That did it for me, I had to say something.

"You must be kidding. You were just smoking a joint last night and now *'Mr. Just Got Saved Baptist'* you're telling me I can't stay here anymore if I continue to sell?" I asked in disbelief.

My dad looked at me and sighed. Then after a brief silence he said,

"David, you have every right to feel the way you do. I know I haven't been the best father figure to you. I was always against going to church with your mom and God's Word, but things are different now. I can't change the past, but we can both start over right now, by doing the right thing."

"Well, I responded, I'm not ready to give up selling. What you want me to do, work at McDonald's making nothing just so that I can say God is happy? Naw, I don't think it takes all that."

"David, I am not saying that, but I cannot have a dealer staying in my house, so you have to make a choice."

"There is no choice. What type of choice are you giving me? Stay here, be broke, and go to Church all the time or sell, get money, and go where I want? Well, I choose selling."

With that parting statement, I went to my room, gathered up my stuff and got ready to leave. To me it really wasn't a big deal because I planned to move soon anyway, but for him to give me an ultimatum was over the top. My dad stopped me at the door and said,

"David, son, please don't do this, you know selling is wrong, I know you do. Your mother drilled the Bible and God's Word in you and I know it's still there."

We stood just looking at each other. I believe my dad saw that I was not backing down and was going to continue to sell. So, with resignation he said,

"David, if you ever give up the game and need to come home, you will always be welcomed. But, son you are living a dangerous life and you need to get out before it's too late. I'll be praying for you."

"Dad, this life is not dangerous at all if you know what you are..."

It was at that moment my gun fell to the floor and we looked at each other. Shamefaced I picked it up and left. I drove around for a little while, still furious because my dad actually put me out. I just couldn't understand how he thought that putting me out was the right thing to do. Did he really think he was helping me? Besides, he had enjoyed the free weed and money he'd gotten; now he wanted to grow a conscience. I kept driving until I got to my Sister Endia's house. My dad had already spoken to her before I got there, because he figured this would be the first place I would go.

"David, dad called and let me know what happened. Do you want to talk about it?"

I stared at her and shook my head no.

"You can stay here as long as you want. I know you will not bring that stuff into my home, and I don't want any of the people you sell with knowing you are here, especially that fool Los. You can let Valencia know because she is a nice girl, but all the rest of them can't come here." She said.

Endia never liked Los. She always felt he was no good because of all the trouble we got into before mom got sick.

"OK and thanks."

I said as I went to my new room to lie down.

16

It was a few days later and I was still in a funk about being kicked out my dad's house. I told Valencia what happened and she tried to tell me not to be mad at my dad. She said he was doing the best he knew how to do. I'll admit I didn't want to hear it, but since it was her, I listened. I had conflicting emotions about the whole situation because I thought my dad should have been in the church with my mom when she was alive. However, she's gone and now he decides it's time for him to get right with GOD. I felt like it was too little too late and insincere. It amazed me to learn that so many people started going to Church after the September 11th disaster. My sister kept saying she was concerned because I looked so down.

One particular day, my sister seemed so excited to see me. I wanted to know what was up.

"David, guess what?!" She said excitedly.

I looked up and waited for her to tell me.

"David, remember how you said you would give anything to see Michael Jordan play again."

I looked at her with a funny expression and tentatively I said, "Yeah."

"Do you still want to see him?" She asked.

"Don't play with me Endia." I shrugged, as I told her; "You know as well as I do that he retired and is not coming back, but if he ever did for even a second I would jump at the chance."

"Well." She said. "Obviously you haven't heard yet, but he is back--with Washington and I have four tickets to see him tomorrow night."

Her smug expression didn't even annoy me as she showed me the tickets. I felt a smile form on my face as everything that was troubling me went out the window as I thought about finally being able to see Jordan live. So, I asked,

"So, how many tickets can I have?"

I said with excitement because Valencia loved Michael Jordan too. She had so many of his shoes and posters I'd have been jealous of how much Valencia liked Jordan if I didn't know how she felt about me.

"Well." Endia replied. "I will give you all of the tickets and I hope you have a good time."

Immediately, I hugged her because Endia always tried to be there for me even though she really didn't have much.

"Thanks. I really appreciate this."

The following night we went to the game, and we arrived at our seats about 30 minutes late because traffic was backed up. Also, since it was not long after 9/11, everyone had to be checked. I took Valencia, Los, and his flavor of the week, to the game. Everyone was excited to see Jordan right there in front of us. I don't know how my sister did it, but we had seats near courtside. When we got to our seats there were some people seated in them, but we asked them to move and they did, so it was no big deal. They began to play the Star Spangled Banner. Everyone in the arena stood silently as the vocalist sang the anthem that is everyone except for Los. It was a surreal moment. But Los being true to himself, remained seated and unembarrassed by the knowledge that he was shown on the overhead screens. They must have had the cameras focused on our section. After looking at the screen further, I noticed Los was looking at Valencia's butt, which ticked me off; however, I chilled because I didn't want to ruin the evening.

We sat down and the game started, seeing Jordan in action made me quickly forget what Los had done. At halftime I said to Valencia,

"Is there anything you want, sweetie."

She smiled and told me what she wanted. Los said sarcastically towards me,

"Sweetie, I want a Coke and a slice of pizza, since you are taking orders."

"Don't hold your breath." I said.

After my reTrey, I walked to get our refreshments. I was returning to my seat when I saw Los hovering over Valencia and then I saw her smack him. I rushed to find out what had happened. Valencia looked upset and Los was red-faced and angry.

"What happened?" I said.

"I want to go." Valencia said angrily.

"Why, baby what happened?!" I asked trying to make sense of what I'd seen.

"Nothing, just take me home." She said as she looked at me.

I hesitated because I wanted to know what happened, but she said.

"David, if you want to stay, that's fine but I've got to get out of here."

Valencia began walking away and Los said,

"Let her go, Dave, she ain't worth it."

I turned and looked at him and I knew he had done something, but I had to catch up with Valencia. I finally caught up with her in the parking lot.

"Baby, what's wrong. What did Los do?" I asked.

"I don't want to talk about it. Just drive me home." She said.

We drove off in silence and about 20 minutes later Valencia began to talk.

"David, I didn't want to tell you what happened because I didn't want you to get upset and get yourself in trouble." She paused, bit her lip, and then continued. "Your boy Los was dogging that girl that he was with, feeling on her and talking to her any type of way. I got tired of seeing and hearing him, so I said that he shouldn't do that to her. He told me it was none of my business and if he wanted to, he would do the same thing to me. So, I told him I wouldn't allow him to. So, he got up and started cursing and saying a lot of stuff about how I was no good for talking to you when he tried first." She paused. "My GOD David, we were kids then, when will he get past that? Anyway, I tried to leave it alone, but he kept getting in my face, even after I told him the next time he gets in my face, I would smack him.

He tried me and got back in my face, so I smacked him, just before you walked up."

I was upset that Los would front my girl like that. Valencia was right not to tell me at the game because I would have lost it knowing Los spoke to her that way. I just couldn't believe my boy Los would come on my girl like that. I mean for him to say she was foul for getting with me after he tried to talk to her, in middle school, indicated he was still upset that Valencia and I are together. I knew, now more than ever, I had to keep my eyes on him.

Los called me a few days after the Jordan game talking like nothing happened that night. I couldn't let it go, so I said,

"Los you were out of order talking to my girl like that. I thought the issue was no longer a problem between us when we talked a little while ago."

"Look." Los answered. "I don't know what you talking about; your girl slapped me because I checked her for getting in my business with that bucket head girl. The only reason I didn't step to her is because I don't waste my time fighting females."

Los obviously forgot how well I know him and was suffering from brain freeze. Dude was the type of guy that would fight male or female for whatever reason. He didn't buy into that a man should never hit a woman. But unlike a lot of those cowardly guys that beat on females, Los was no coward and he would take on all comers. So, I said,

"Yeah, whatever man. So, what did you want?"

I asked while realizing that Los lied about Valencia and knowing I had to watch my back with him. He went on to talk about stuff that didn't amount to anything. What he was trying to do was feel me out and get information on my relationship with Valencia. Los knew if Valencia told me everything that went down that, he didn't have a chance with her and that she was really into me. He was clueless to the fact that he didn't have a chance regardless because Valencia simply couldn't stand him. I listened to him and didn't show any sign that I knew he was lying. The one thing my dad did teach me was,

"Keep your friends close and your enemies even closer."

Now that I definitely knew where Los was coming from, I knew he couldn't be trusted.

Things started to get back to normal around October. School was open and once again, we were moving product. The money was rolling in. But, like I said, things just weren't the same between Los and me. When I saw him, he complained about how broke he was. I couldn't understand why he was always so broke. After all, business was interrupted for only a few weeks, so he shouldn't have been that low on funds. Nevertheless, he gave the best performance, like he was two steps from a refrigerator box in the alley.

After everything started to settle a little we were able to get more weed to sell. But there were changes made at the college that made it more difficult to sell. We had to be more careful because security was changed and amped up to protect the campus from terrorists, which affected our business. Sales were cut in half as a result, and a lot of our customers were not as carefree as they used to be. The 9/11 tragedy affected our customers in various ways. There was a huge amount of former customers who all of a sudden felt patriotic and joined the military. Then there was the group who decided they needed to change their lives and stop wasting it by smoking weed. Still others became Christians and would not smoke because of their newfound faith in God. So, our earnings dropped from $700 a day to $350 a day. Though this wasn't the best, it still was cool. I made do. I had to cut back on certain things but I still made out.

Los was surprisingly quiet and content. He kept saying he was happy to be making bread again. He said that those weeks of not earning money hurt but he didn't care about the cut, he just had to deal with it. I guess he felt like a little money was better than none. Although Los was still a little flashy, he kinda chilled on all the women he usually hung with. I really didn't see him with anybody except Kelly, and that was mainly out at the club. I noticed that he was not hanging as much with the other fellas either. But, I simply dismissed it and didn't concern myself with it. Nonetheless, Los was not about to settle for just half of what he used to earn. I knew him and it was only matter or time before he would want and need to regain his losses. I knew that something was about to go down with him. So, his act was unconvincing for me. I knew he was plotting something, but I didn't know what.

I really realized how sneaky and dirty Los was when he tried to play me with Valencia. All these years, I convinced myself that we were like brothers, but now that Los was coming into his own he showed his true colors. Los felt that if he couldn't get what he wanted, nobody else should have it either, even if he had to stab me in the back. This betrayal by Los allowed me to understand what was meant by an old German proverb that states,

"Better an honest enemy than a false friend."

18

I heard once that, "In the midst of confusion, there is opportunity." It was the last day of the school semester and I went to make my drop. Once again we were earning the kind of money we were earning before the 9/11 disaster. However, it took more work to make the $700 a day we were used to.

One particular day, it was cold and snowy, and I noticed a lot of cop cars at our drop spot. I pulled to the side and remained out of sight to watch what was happening. I was shivering a little bit because the heat had gone out in my car. I sat and waited as I observed the flashing police lights and the officers who had Trey stretched out on the hood of his car. The cops had him in all that snow with no coat on so I knew the brother was freezing. They put the silver bracelets on him and took him away. Ant made a few comments, but there was nothing he could do. As he was driven away, Trey kept proclaiming,

"How was I supposed to know?! Y'all don't have no proof!"

Most people probably thought he'd been arrested for drug possession, but I knew different simply because Ant and Trey never kept product at the spot. They only used this place to drop money. They always sent us someplace else to pick up the weed.

After the cops left, I pulled up, got out the car, and Ant began to talk. He said,

"I can't believe this is how my man is going down. All because of a girl! A girl! He's out because of a female!"

"What are you talking about?"

"Didn't you hear me?!" Ant said irritated. "They just took Trey away for Statutory Rape." He looked at me and continued. "Tina just had that baby and named Trey as the father."

"Wait a minute, why did she dime him out?"

"I don't know, but I know it had to be Tina because she was the only underage girl he fooled with." He continued to pace, and talk to himself.

"I thought her parents had to press charges for him to get Stat Rape."

"Man, this is an upcoming election year and 9/11 is still fresh in people's minds, especially that prosecutor who's running for

Mayor. She has been campaigning on the idea that young people need to be protected against predators. So, she has stepped up her efforts to bring Stat Rape cases to trial trying to prove she's doing something. Man, and they got him good, one test of that baby and he's done. He's looking at about 15 years unless he cuts a deal. But, either way he's done out here."

I couldn't understand how Ant would cut his boy loose like that, but hey, this is how it goes in the game. Sometimes you have to put friendship to the side when your friend becomes a liability to your business.

A couple weeks went by and I didn't hear anything about Trey. But, Ant was on point, because in a matter of weeks, Trey cut a deal and got 1-2 years for Stat Rape. He wanted to fight it but his lawyer told him to take the deal seeing that he was a DNA test and a campaign commercial away from serving some serious time. After he thought about it, he didn't want to take the chance of becoming the poster boy for the prosecutor's campaign against crime, so he quickly cut a deal. Ant was left to manage alone which meant he needed to find someone to step into Trey's place very soon. That's the thing about the game, you could be killed, jailed or hurting, but everything continues to go on without you. Things would never be the same again. I knew that this was the beginning of the end.

19

As soon as Ant got wind of Trey's deal, he arranged to meet with Los and me. When we arrived at the spot, Ant looked upset and a little uneasy that his right-hand man was gone. Aside from Trey, we were the only ones that worked for him that had it together. All the rest of his workers either were smoking weed themselves or using other drugs. Los and I kept it professional, strictly adhering to the rule that the rap group NWA said;

"Don't get high on your own supply."

Ant said,

"Trey got 1 to 2 years and probably can get out in 6 months, but he's done out here."

"Why do you say that? He'll only be gone half a year?" I asked.

"We stay under the radar." He paused. "Having Trey with us would bring too much attention. They keep more tabs on a sex offender than they do any other criminal. On top of that, everybody is looking at Trey for the murders of Tina and that social worker. The cops would be all over us and I'm not willing to risk it, so he's done. Which brings me to why I called you two, with Trey gone I have to make a lot of changes. Both of you have worked with me for a while now and I need one of you to take his place. We just got things back to normal and I plan on keeping it that way. I can't afford to put anyone in Trey's position who can't handle it. Of the two of you . . ."

Ant was still speaking as I delved into my thoughts. I could see the anticipation in Los' eyes as Ant was about to say who would replace Trey. It really didn't matter to me because I was ok with the $700 a day I made and it wasn't like I planned to do this forever. Los had more invested in the game than I did. He wanted this position so he could eventually make some moves of his own. I found out a few weeks after Trey went down that Los had set him up. Like, I said everyone in the hood knew about Tina. Los knew that Trey distanced himself from her and played on that because he knew if she talked, Trey would be out of the way.

By using Tina, Los didn't have to worry about Ant retaliating against him for setting up his boy. I found out that Tina got pressured from her parents to reveal who the father was to get more money from the state. Since, Tina was underage the money the state gave her would actually be added to her parents' check. But the state required the father's information be provided to collect child support from the father if possible. Also, Cynthia, the caseworker for Tina's family, knew Trey from the club, so as soon as Tina revealed Trey was the father, Cynthia filed a report on him, based on his age. Cynthia and Los' girl Kelly were friends as well as colleagues, so Los used this relationship to pay Cynthia $5000 to report Trey. That is why Los was complaining about being so broke when we couldn't sell. He spent his most of his money arranging this whole set up.

It was the perfect set up, but what Los didn't anticipate was that Kelly had a big mouth when she got drunk. After she'd had a few too many Kelly told me everything. I had to admit Los was quite devious with how he manipulated his plan. It also let me know that Los wanted to be the man on top at whatever cost. Tina, Kelly, and Cynthia didn't know that Los never left any loose ends. He had to get rid of them all in order to keep his actions a secret. Los was ready to step out on his own to make a name for himself. He thought using Tina was the best way to set his plan in motion. As for Cynthia, in everybody's eyes it would appear she was only trying to protect her client from the big bad black guy who crossed the line. No one ever suspected the women were the victims of Los' calculated plan to get Trey out of the picture. Poor Tina, Kelly, and Cynthia didn't figure out they were being used, therefore, they got caught up in Los' quest for money and power. They never realized their days were numbered. Los could not take the chance that they would keep quiet about his role in getting Trey arrested so he had to kill them to silence them. He knew that Ant would either kill him or cut him off, either way he would be done.

The women were killed within days of each other just after Trey copped to a plea. I put the pieces together as I remembered my last serious conversation with Los. The drug game had turned Los into a cold, calculating, heartless person I no longer recognized. I was seeing my old friend in a new light with a sinister glow; he not only was a backstabber, but a heartless, money and power hungry murderer as well. Los was willing to kill three young women to propel himself to a higher level in the game. He was determined to get what he wanted even if he had to commit murder to do it. Such knowledge is why I never let on that I knew what he'd done. If he wanted me to know, he would have told me. Anyone who had knowledge of what he'd done or just managed to find out, as I did, became a potential target, not just for Los, but for Ant as well. Again, Ant would have killed Los for setting up Trey, and anyone else who knew about the plan and didn't tell him. Los' greed continued to grow and was becoming deadlier for all associated with him. All he ever talked about was how he was going to be the man one day and give the orders. He had the car, the workers, the money, and the women, but he didn't have the connection, when he got that, he said, it would be on.

Everything Los wanted seemed to be within his reach, with Trey being sent away to prison. He even knew that Ant wouldn't bring Trey back because as a sex offender he had to register his location, the law keeps a close eye on sex offenders, and everybody associated with them. Also, they would keep an even closer eye on him when he got out because they would suspect he had a hand in Tina's, Kelly's, and Cynthia's murders. Ant didn't need this kind of attention. Even though Trey was his boy, it was nothing personal, it was strictly business.

Bringing me out of my reflection, Ant continued,

"….that is why I made my decision." He paused. "David, I want you to step into Trey's place."

Following that announcement, it was so silent I could hear the proverbial pin hit the ground. I felt like I was having an out of body experience, I was standing here, and yet I wasn't. I'm sure

you know the feeling. The thought didn't even occur to me that
he would want me to fill Trey's shoes. I didn't know what to
think and I knew Los was not too happy about that, seemingly
out of the blue, I was chosen over him. Now, Los had to report
to me. Still, Ant continued,

"Los, I want you to see if you could find someone else at the
college that can partner up with you."

Los looked at me with a blank and somewhat angry
expression before he looked at Ant. I could tell Los was not
ready for me to be next in line and him still be a runner. We both
thought he would be Ant's choice because he had been selling
longer than I had; he recruited others to work, and he was willing
to sell more weed than I was. So, I said,

"Ant, are you sure about this? My man Los here is who you
want. You know I'm not going to be in the life much longer."

Ant looked up as he said,

"David let me talk to you for a few minutes. Los, I'll catch
you later."

Still in disbelief, Los was frozen in place. He was still
seething because the position he wanted and needed for so long,
the position he thought was within his grasp, had been given
away. He would have remained, if Ant hadn't said,

"Los, I said, see you later!"

Hearing the steel in Ant's tone, Los composed himself, began
to walk away, and said,

"Alright, Dave, I'll catch up with you soon."

After he left, Ant waited a second and started explaining why
he chose me over Los.

"Let me explain something to you. In this business, you can't
have a hot dog running your business. David you have a cooler
head than Los. The fact that you're only doing this for a little
while lets me know you won't take any unnecessary risks. You
are all about business. I've been watching how you do things--

you sell and get out of dodge. You even put more in your bags to sell them faster even though you make less money."

"How did you know I did that?" I asked in surprise.

"I keep tabs on all the people that work for me. You were smart to pay off the guards on campus who are on duty during the times you sell. It's that sort of initiative, which sets you apart. Trey was the same way. He only stayed in the drug game to help me, not because he wanted to or even had to." He paused for a moment then continued. "On the other hand, your boy Los is too flashy and feels he has to prove something. He works for me, and yet he drives a more expensive car than I do and pays more for his clothes, drawing too much attention. Remember, we stay under the radar and we won't even talk about the women he fools with."

I thought about what he said, but I felt a need to remind him that I was not going to be in the game much longer.

"Yeah, I know what you mean about Los, but remember a few months ago I let you know in six months when I graduate, I'm out."

Ant smiled as he looked at me and said,

"That's another reason I chose you, because I know that you are not trying to take over the operation. You are actually the perfect worker, you don't ask too many questions; you never try to advance beyond where you are. You just do your work and leave it alone. I like that. So many guys I know say they want out, but they do stupid stuff to make it impossible for them to leave." He paused. "I'm not going to get in your way. I just need you to step in for a little while until I get someone else. You know I don't play games, so it will just be a little while."

Ant sighed and seemed to drift off. It seemed that all of a sudden he went into deep reflection and began to speak,

"I'm getting tired out here. People don't understand when you are on top everybody wants what you got and you can't make a mistake or it will be your last. I know you and Los are boys, but I can also see that you are not as close as you were when you first started." He paused. "David, I'm going to warn you, you better watch him."

For the first time, I really looked at Ant and he appeared tired and worn out. But, I took heed to what he said. I was a little surprised he shared his concern for me, but I knew he was right. Knowing Los, he was not going to let this setback of not getting Trey's position stop him from achieving his goal.

20

For the next few weeks, Ant taught me the ropes of Trey's position. I'll admit I had it made. All I had to do was set up the time to meet the runners for their drops, set up where they picked up their new supply, and let Ant know if there were any problems. This was a lot better and easier than selling at the college or anywhere else. I started making a little over a $1000 a day, which suited me fine. I continued to stack my loot. Los continued to spend his money on cars, clothes, jewelry, and women. I had saved a little over $60,000. I was trying to stack my loot because I knew that my time to get out of the game was close. I was already a little tired in this game. True, we made money, but it was tiring because you had to continue to watch your back. You just never knew who may be plotting against you.

Also, facing the reality of the change in my relationship with Los was a bit overwhelming at times. When Los killed Tina it did something to me, knowing that my one-time best friend had become a murderer was unreal. I mean this was my boy, who I've known since we were little kids and now I don't know who he is or what he'll do next. I felt uneasy around him because I didn't know if I would be next on his agenda. I kept thinking about how Tina's child growing up without knowing his mother. As painful as it was to lose my mom at 17, I couldn't imagine not knowing her at all. I have many memories of her, but Tina's child will only know what people say about her. I wouldn't wish that on anybody and for Los to take Tina's life before her baby could know her, was just plain heartless. I had misjudged the length to which Los was willing to go to get ahead in the game. I willingly admit I am not cut out for his level of treachery. My attitude is live and let live, so I started working my exit plan.

Ant recognized the signs that my time in the game was almost up, because he constantly told me he envied the fact that I was making a way to get out and have a normal life. Ant knew his life and fortune were wrapped up in the game, it was all he had.

He dropped out of school in the ninth grade and didn't look back. Now at 25 years old, with no skills and barely able to read, in his mind he was stuck. However, the one thing I appreciated about him is he never tried to get in anybody's way when they wanted to get out. Because Ant knew I was not a threat to him, he brought me to meet his connect. I met him, but I still kept my distance. One thing about this game is that the more you know the more likely you will die or be stuck in it. I was determined neither option would be my fate.

After I took over Trey's position, Los and I didn't speak much with each other anymore. He picked up his stuff and made his drop. I tried to talk with him, but he was evasive and told me he'd better get to work or I would tell Ant. Los was still upset for having to report to me. He could not comprehend not standing in my place after all the energy and effort he'd put into getting rid of Trey. I knew he was biding his time before he made his next move. I tried to overlook him knowing I would be out soon and I didn't want any conflict my last few months in the game. I realized the relationship I used to have with Los was based on the fact that we were both down and equals. But, now that I had a position higher than he did, Los had a hard time accepting that.

But, as time moved on the money was flowing. Ant kept saying how much he wished I wasn't going because he liked how I did things. He liked that I didn't ask too many questions and was not all up in his connect's face. He appreciated that I talked with him and got his okay first, before I made any major moves. I was just biding my time, two months had past and shortly, I would be out. To keep the cops happy, I had to grease a few palms. It cost quite a bit more than before 9/11, but still it worked out. Ant wanted to make up for all the money that was being spent to keep the cops off us, so he hired a few more workers. It was about six of us before and now we were up to ten, including Ant and myself. I could tell having more workers didn't sit right with Los initially, because he thought I was making more while his earnings remained unchanged. In his mind, more workers meant even less money for him.

Being in Trey's old position also meant I had to frequent the club to keep my ear to the street. Remember, the club is where mostly everybody hung out, so it made perfect business sense that one of us, Ant or myself, would be there. This put me in the position where I had frequent run-ins with Los. He really didn't say much except for the few times he tried to get information out of me when he saw me and Valencia at the club. He kept asking me if I saw the connect and who he was. Mistakenly, I let him know that I had met the connect, but I wouldn't tell him who he was and where we met him. Though, I didn't come flat out and say I met the connect I implied it when I told him;

"I'm in Trey's position, what do you think?"

Los started chiding me, with statements like,

"Oh, you big time now. So, you can't tell your boy nothing anymore. You're too big for me now."

I just let him talk. I wasn't about to mess myself up getting involved in his power hungry plot to try to get the connect so he could step out on his own. I learned, however, when there is no opportunity, some people will create one.

21

One night Valencia and I were out together, when I got a call
on my cell. I didn't answer it right away, because I saw it was
Los. I decided to return his call and said,
"What's up?"
He was quiet. Again, I said,
"Los, what's up? Is everything alright?"
Los sighed heavily,
"Dave, my dad is dead. I just left the hospital. The doctors
said that he died with a needle in his arm."
I felt numb. Even though I was not close to his dad or Los
anymore for that matter, but the pain of losing a parent was still
fresh, so I felt for him.
"Man, I don't know what to say, I'm so sorry. Is there
anything I can do?"
Valencia knew I was talking to Los and gave me a grim look
like she was going to kill me for being this nice to him. So, I
hurried to reply to what Los was telling me,
"Yeah Los, you'll call me once you made the funeral
arrangements for your father. Alright, talk to you later."
After I hung up, Valencia responded supportively,
"David, I'm sorry, I didn't know. I feel awful. I should have
known you had good reason to be so nice."
"It's ok. With what happened between the two of you, I
understand."
I said as I drifted in thought. All I could think is Los didn't
have a mother or father now. How tough could that be? I still
have my dad even though we're not on the best terms, but at least
we have a chance to work things out between us.
The funeral was very small. Los' dad didn't have many
friends or relatives. It was short and simple. When Los saw me,
he hugged me and we talked.
"David, you're all I have left. I know things between us have
been rocky lately and it has been my fault. So, I'm sorry to you
and Valencia."

"That's alright." I said.

Los started to cry. Seeing his pain tore through me and took the fight out of me. At that moment, I forgave him for everything that went down between us and we continued to talk.

"Los, man it's time to start seriously thinking about getting out of the game. I don't want to be in a casket anytime soon and I know you don't either."

"Yeah, you right." He paused. "David, I hope that we can be boys again. Like I said you're all I got."

As he wiped his tear from his face, I said,

"Man, you know we . . . ."

I was interrupted by my cell, I looked at the number and it was Tony, one of the runners. So, I answered it.

"Tony, I'm at Los' father's funeral, what do you want?"

"Ant is dead. Somebody shot him…"

"Wait a minute, what did you just say?"

I couldn't believe it. First Trey goes to prison, now Ant's dead. I looked at Los and I must admit my first thought was that Los killed him or had him killed, but I forced myself to dismiss such a disturbing thought. Surely, he wasn't that devious, for God's sake, dude has just lost his father. Tony said a few more things, but I didn't even hear him, I was still trying to wrap my mind around Ant's death. As Tony hung up the phone, the last thing I heard him say was,

"OK, boss."

This is what he always said to Ant. I felt like I had just been slammed against a wall as it dawned on me that I was now the top guy. The game for me had just changed and became more difficult for me to get out. The sudden revelation devastated me. Los tried to talk to me, but I had to get out of there. I jumped in my car and rode around until I stopped at the park where Los and I played as little kids. I started to daydream about us playing basketball and talking trash on the court, when I felt a hand on my shoulder. A little startled, I looked up and saw the bum that Los dogged out a little while ago.

"Young blood, how are you?"

"Fine, I guess." I said half-heartedly.

He looked at me, smiled, and then said,

"I see you're a little down, but remember young blood God loves you. Whatever trouble you are in or about to face, don't give up on God, he can help you. Look at me, I gave up on him and look where I'm at."

What he said reminded me of my mother who always said stuff like that.

"There's probably a lot of stuff you don't understand right now, but remember if you ever get into a bad situation, pray and God will make a way."

I couldn't say anything because at that moment what he said was a painful reminder of my mother's last words to me.

A couple days after Ant was killed I had everything up and running. I already knew the set up and had the money to pay the connect to keep things going. Ant showed me where he kept the stash of cash he used to pay the connect because he didn't believe in credit. He always said,

"That's how people get killed; they always owe the person above them and can't pay. I mean what happens if you get robbed or busted? They still want their money and if you don't have it, you get killed and in the garbage bags you go."

So, he always paid up front and didn't have to worry about that. But, still, he was killed. I couldn't handle the business alone and there was no one among the men I could trust, so I had to utilize Los. He was so happy to be in Trey's old position. I knew he figured he would get the connect and start his own thing. But, he didn't anticipate that the connect wouldn't even do business until he got to know you. He only did business with me so fast because he knew my dad. As it turned out, he was owner of the car lot where I bought my car. Los on the other hand, was required to stay outside while I conducted business with him. Again, Los felt he was close, yet so far from getting what he wanted. As for myself, I was still two months away from being free, so it didn't really matter that Los wanted to do his own thing. But, I soon learned, in this business the worst thing you can be is careless.

22

Valencia and I were studying for finals. Semester finals were almost over, and we decided to study at my new apartment. I had to pay the landlady a full year's rent for her to let me get this place, but I liked it, so it was cool. I made sure that nobody knew where I lived besides Valencia and my immediate family. I couldn't take the chance of anyone else knowing, not even Los. I wanted to start distancing myself from this life, so not letting the fellas know where I lived limited their access to me. In a few months, I would be leaving with Valencia to attend college out of state. I would be leaving my past behind me, and hopefully beginning my future with Valencia. I made sure to keep my grades up so that I could go anywhere she went. I truly loved this girl and I couldn't imagine my life without her. We have been together for over two years, and my feelings for her were stronger than ever. I kept looking at her as we worked. She smiled and told me to keep studying. Finally, I said,

"Valencia, I need to talk to you."

Looking concerned, she said,

"What's wrong?"

I paused as I looked at her and said,

"We've been together for over two years and my life has really been good since I've been with you. After my mom died, I never thought I could feel this close to anyone again. I want to ask..."

As I got on my knee and pulled out the ring, Endia helped me find,

"Will you marry me?"

Her face dropped, she smiled and then frowned. Her reaction puzzled me for a moment.

"David, as much as I would like to, I can't marry a drug dealer." She continued speaking as she looked at me. "David, I have to say this." She paused. "Our relationship has gone as far as it's going to go. You know that and so do I. Your proposal tonight potentially moves our relationship to a whole new height, becoming husband and wife. I just can't do it. Regardless that you only sell weed, it's still drugs, and I still worry about you.

Think about all the guys you hang around and the kinds of activities they're involved in, especially that fool Los. I can't go through life worrying if something is going to happen to my husband."

She said while tearing up and I saw the pain in her eyes. I heard the agony in her voice. I knew that our relationship was at a pivotal point and it was time for me to make a decision.

"David, you have to make a decision right now, it's either me or the game."

She stood waiting for my answer. Valencia was the type that only gave a man one chance when it came to matters of the heart. I knew that she would not agree to my continuing to sell drugs. I knew by choosing to sell, I would be placing my business above her, above us. Also, since Ant was killed, I knew all the fellas were depending on me to keep everything together. I planned to hook up Los with the connect, but somehow, I knew the connect wouldn't do business with him. He'd only just allowed Los to meet him a week ago. So, if I walk away now, everything will shut down. I know Los and this would not sit well with him, but I can't allow Valencia to get away. I know I would be miserable without her. I'd be an empty shell of a man for the rest of my life. Valencia filled the void left by my mother's death and I needed to fill the emptiness inside me. So, I said,

"Valencia, I have no choice, you are all I want." I paused. "If leaving the game is what it takes to keep you in my life, then so be it." I said.

She looked at me, hugged me, put the ring on, and said,

"David, I love you and of course I will marry you." She paused. "But, I'm giving you a month to handle your business. If you can't, then I have to move on because I can't handle losing you."

With her final statement, I held her and knew that my time in the game was over.

23

Two weeks had passed and I felt it was time to start making my move to break away from this life. As I drove to the spot where the connect was I kept rehearsing in my head what I was going to say. With Ant dead, Trey in jail, and no one to replace me, I just knew the connect would make it hard for me to get out. I don't know many people who would willingly give up an easy $40,000 a week. See, a lot of guys don't realize when you become the leader of a crew it's nearly impossible to just walk away. Until Ant got killed, my plan was to exit with *him* still on top. Then after Ant was killed, I thought I could get out by getting Los to step in, but the connect wouldn't even allow him into the same room with us. The connect's actions spoke loud and clear, he would never do business with Los. The thought of what Ant said about Los kept ringing in my head,

"He's a hotdog and flashy."

So, I know if Ant could read Los so well, there's no way the connect couldn't. I know a lot of people not involved in the game think that I could just walk away and say nothing, but only a fool would just pack up and leave knowing he'd always have to watch his back. I refused to live like that and I wouldn't allow Valencia to live like that either. So, here I was about to walk into the lion's den.

After being patted down, I walked in with a bag holding $80,000. I figured giving the connect two weeks of money upfront would ease the tension of my exiting. The connect motioned for me to sit down. I sat directly across from him and started to speak.

"I really need to talk with you in private."

"Who do you think you are coming in here demanding private time with the boss? Fool, you know people have been killed for less."

He said while reaching for his gun. The connect motioned for him to stop and said.

"So, you have something to tell me in private huh. This better be good." He paused. "All of you just wait by the door, I'm curious to hear what the young playa's got to say."

"But boss!"

"It's alright. Just wait at the door."

As the men left, one of them turned and said to me.

"If you try anything, you're mine."

The connect looked at me and said;

"So, what is it that's so important that you need to talk to me alone?"

I started to tremble inside because I didn't know how he would react to what I had to say. First, I handed him the bag with $80,000 in it, as he opened the bag I said,

"I'm bringing you this $80,000 because I want out, I'm done, and I'm ready to move on with my life."

I looked at him waiting, trying to read his expression, but he simply smiled and shook his head. His smile didn't put me at ease, if anything it made me even more nervous, so much so that I could feel my heart pounding in my throat. After what seemed like an eternity, he said,

"David or should I say "Little Davie?"

He said with a smile. I was at a loss because only my family and Valencia called me that, even Los didn't know that name. He continued,

"David, I know a lot more about you than you can ever imagine." He paused, studied my expression and continued. "I guess your dad never told you about his past." He shook his head. "Back in the day your dad and I used to sell together. With each of us being an only child, we were like brothers. We sold and made lots of money."

I was completely perplexed, thinking about the man who raised me and judging him against the man he was talking about. Totally confused, I listened as he continued.

"That was until he met your mother. Your dad fell hard for her; she was different, not like all the other people we were used to. She actually cared for him and not his money. He always had to be close to her, and I had never seen your dad act like that over a woman before, but I started to see less and less of him until he married her."

"I'm sorry but I can't even recognize the man you're describing right now as my dad, first of all, he's always broke." I interrupted

He leaned back, laughed, and continued.

"Your mom had been pressing your dad to get out because she already had two kids and was about to have a third--you. Your dad stayed in the business out of loyalty to me. We were the best crack dealers on the street."

"A couple nights before you were born, one of our rivals shot up the house we dealt out of and nearly killed me, but your father took a bullet for me. I never forgot what he did for me. After that, he was done and I couldn't blame him. Out of love for me, your dad made me your godfather. Why do you think I gave you that car for $2000?" He paused as I sat there in complete shock. My godfather continued. Over the years, I stopped selling crack and got into selling weed. I offered your dad money, but he wouldn't take it." He paused. "He's still my brother and you are still my godson. I wouldn't come around because of the life your mom and dad tried to build together for all of you kids. I still kept an eye on y'all and when I found out who raped your mom, he was taken care of."

There was silence as I realized how much my godfather had kept tabs on us. But, he continued.

"David, I figured you were trying to get out when you started to distance yourself from everything. That fool Los, is a snake and you've got to watch him. He will never be a part of my inner circle. I know he had Ant and those women killed and set up Trey on the Stat Rape case. Knowing what I know, he will never be allowed to get close enough to stab me in the back."

Again, I was perplexed. How could he know what Los had done? My confusion must have shown on my face, because He said,

"David, I've been in the game too long not to know what's happening on the street. I always keep tabs on the people who work for me and on the people, I supply. Los played the game real close. He thought by eliminating Ant, you would be the one on top and all he had to do was get to me, watch you leave, and everything would be his. But the player got played." My 'godfather' continued, "Guys like him are too smart for their own good, and can't think beyond their own ambitions. Never once did he think that I would not meet him." He paused, looked at his watch and continued. "David, this is the longest I've talked to you. Though I hadn't seen you since you were a baby, I love you like you were my own but I can't show any affection toward you. If anybody knew my fondness for you or your dad, your whole family would be in danger. I chose this life and I have to live with it, but you don't. Tell your dad I said hello and though we don't run together anymore, I've still got his back. Know that I'm letting you get out because of my love for him. Now son, I am about to hit you and when I hit you, stay on the ground until I tell you to get up; and David don't come here again."

I nodded, then he hit me and I fell. I wasn't even pretending. My godfather clocked me so hard, I didn't see just stars, I saw a whole galaxy. He said don't get up until he told me, that was no problem because, I was too dazed to get up. His men rushed in and he said,

"Get this fool out of here!"

He picked up my bag and threw it back at me.

"I don't want him around here anymore."

One of his men was pulling out his gun.

"Naw, let this fool alone, just throw him out."

His men grabbed me and threw me out, laughing. Yeah, I was bleeding a little, but I was free. My dad had saved the connect's life which saved my life, as well. It's crazy how some things work out. My mother always said that the Lord worked in mysterious ways. She used to say that our family was blessed because she was in church. She always quoted,

"The just man walketh in his integrity: his children are blessed after him. Proverbs 20:7. "

I knew that it could not have been anyone but God, who allowed this to work out. All I could say within myself was,

"Thanks Ma and Dad."

24

"You want to what?!"

Los said in disbelief. I went to see him after leaving the connect. I told him,

"Los, I'm out. It's my time, I'm done."

I gave him a bag with $40,000 in it.

"I know this is all of a sudden, but here, this money should sustain you for a while."

Los looked at me with anger in his eyes as he opened the bag and saw the money. His disposition changed a bit, but still, he looked hopeless because he knew without me his chances with the connect were shot. I continued with what I was saying,

"I'm not leaving you empty handed. So, take the money and make it work, but I'm done."

He looked up from the bag of money and said,

"So, let me guess, Valencia wants you out, huh?"

"Los I have been telling you for so long that my time in the game was temporary. I don't know why you keep blaming Valencia for my decision."

"You're letting this gold mine go for a woman. You crazy, but I can dig it." Los said like he didn't hear me.

"Man like I said you knew my plan all along was to make enough money, then to get out, so now I'm done."

He looked at me, shook my hand, pulled me in for a half hug, and picked up the bag of money. Los said,

"So, what you bout to get into?"

"I'm going to my dad's, I just want to let him know I'm done out here."

"I know he will be happy." Los paused for a moment and said, "Well I'm gone, hit me up later."

I simply smiled and said nothing. I was a little surprised at how uneventful the conversation turned out to be. I thought I would have to tell Los that I had already severed ties with the connect, but I said nothing, he'd find out soon enough.

25

I walked in my dad's house and boy had it changed. There were no ashtrays, no liquor, and he was playing gospel music. We sat down and began to talk,

"Dad, a lot has changed since the last time I was here."

"Yeah, you're right. The Lord has changed me inside and out." He said with a smile.

"I have some things I need to tell you, but first my godfather said hello."

I was totally amused by the shock on his face. He begin to say,

"How?"

"Yeah dad, I know who he is, and he told me about you and mom. He told me this as I was getting out the game. I realized I couldn't stay in the game and be with Valencia too, so I had to let it go."

My dad started praising God and said,

"Praise The Lord, your mother would be so happy."

"Yeah, and thanks to you I was able to walk away. If you hadn't taken that bullet, I might be dead right now." I said.

"He told you that, huh?" He paused. "Yeah I was a cut up back in the day and did a lot of dirt, but God pulled me out, though at that time, I didn't recognize it was Him, and He's done it for you too." He paused. "David you need to get right with God. It's a true blessing that you are out of the game, but now you have to think about your soul."

I have to admit, I didn't come to hear a sermon, but I listened as he talked about Jesus dying and raising again.

"I know you've heard this before, but what good is it for you to get out the game, live a good life with Valencia, then die and go to hell. Most people are fearful of a lot of things, but if they stopped and realized what real fear is, they would change their life."

I leaned in and said,

"Real fear. What real fear are you talking about?" I asked.

He started talking to me about the rich man and Lazarus and stressed this one point in the scripture,

"And in hell he lift up his eyes, being in torments...." Luke 16:23

For the first time I actually felt fear come over me because I never had it put to me quite like that before. Just thinking about what he said about real fear made me realize that he was right and I kept hearing my mother quoting the Bible;

"What does it profit a man to gain the whole world and lose his own soul, and what can a man give in exchange for his soul." Matthew 16:26.

I would have the money, the woman, and the life, but until I got right with God, hell would be my home. This kept running through my head as I drove home that night. It made sense to me that it was time for me to change all areas of my life. I had spent a lot of time looking out for my physical, emotional, and even my financial wellbeing, but what about my spiritual wellbeing? Somehow, it made sense to me that my spiritual life was just as important as my natural life. Yeah, I needed to be right with God. As I turned the corner, my cell phone rang and I noticed it was Valencia's number. I answered it and said,

"Hey Baby, what's up?"

"David, is that you?!"

The voice on the other end sounded like her roommate, but her voice was too frantic and I couldn't tell.

"What's wrong?" I asked knowing something was up since she was using Valencia's phone.

"You need to get here quick, Valencia's hurt and she's asking for you."

"Hurt? What happened?" I asked.

"She's been beat real bad and she keeps asking for you, David please hurry up and get here!"

I raced through the city streets like a mad man. I had to get there. I wasn't worried about no cops because they never were around the hood anyway. I pulled up and jumped out the car, leaving my door open, in my urgency to get to Valencia.

As soon as I walked in, I saw Valencia lying on the floor, her life's blood pooled around her as she turned to me. Coughing up blood and her voice cracking, she said,

"David, I knew you would come."

As I kneeled down next to her, I felt myself tremble as I asked,

"Who did this to you?"

I was fighting to keep my composure but I was losing the battle and swiftly. I was so numb, I felt like I was dying. She said as best she could while still coughing,

"I came home,".... Gasping for breath as she continued... "from your place and I was... walking to the door... when... someone... pushed me.... from behind into.... the house. He ripped....my clothes.... and tried.... to rape me, but I.... kneed him. He....kept saying"...as she continued to gasp for breath, "he was going....to kill me. He.... kept saying he.... was going to kill me.... if I wasn't in the way.... he would have everything."

She coughed up a little blood and I wiped her face with the towel her roommate had placed beside her.

"I scratched.... and bit him, she cried, but he kept.... hitting me.... and started choking me.... and kept.... choking me saying.... he was going.... to kill me. Valencia sobbed. "He grabbed me....and slammed.... my head....into.... the coffee table. Everything went black." She said while coughing.

Her roommate said,

"I found her lying here unconscious and bleeding. I guess the guy heard my car and ran out. I shook her and threw water in her face until she woke up coughing."

"Did you see who it was?!"

"No, I didn't."

Valencia then said,

"I didn't see....his face....it was....but.... I.... knew his voice." She coughed and then said,

"David....it was....Los!" she cried.

26

"It's my fault!"

I kept saying to myself as visions of Valencia beaten, bruised, and bleeding flashed through my mind. I should have never given Los the heads up on my exit from the game. I had just handed this fool $40,000 free and clear, and this is how he repays me by trying to kill and rape my woman? I knew at that moment I had to take him out or I would never have a chance at a normal life. As soon as Los found out Valencia was alive, he would no doubt try to kill us both, so I had to play this cool. I had to throw Los off guard and make void his suspicions, so I called him crying. I told him that Valencia was dead.

"Los, I don't care how long it takes I got to get this fool. First, I lose my mother and now Valencia. I can't let this go. I need you to do me a favor. I already called Tony and Don. I need you to call everybody else and tell them to meet me at the warehouse, right now. I need all y'all to help me find out who killed my girl."

"Dave, calm down. You said you're out of the game, man, let me take care of this for you."

"Los, I'm not trying to hear you. I've got to handle my business. You just get everybody else out here, alright?" I said angrily.

"Alright." He said.

Tony and Don was already there waiting for me. We sat around for about twenty minutes. They kept asking me what was so urgent that we had to meet tonight. I told them we would talk about it once everybody else came in. The warehouse was one of the places we kept weed for people to pick up. It was an abandoned two-story building with an illegal electrical hook up. Everybody had to come through the front because the back door was blocked by a big dumpster. So, basically, it was one way in and out. I preferred this location because this was the perfect spot to take out Los. Not too many people lived in the area, so I didn't have to worry about witnesses. We were meeting on the second floor; the first floor was too accessible to bums or homeless people wandering about.

Los and the rest of the crew finally walked in. It was nine of us counting me and Los. As soon as they came up the stairs, I started to speak.

"Tonight someone attacked and killed my girl."

Everybody looked at each other and started talking about how they were going to find and kill that fool. Los was playing along, giving the performance of his life, talking about how he was going to be the one to take this guy out because of what he did to Valencia.

"Let me get my hands on him, he's gonna pay for hurting my man's girl. You know we go way back. You hurt, I hurt. He ain't gone know what hit him."

"Yeah, I got something real proper live for that fool." I said playing along.

I pulled out my weapon, a silver 9mm, for everybody to see. Then I turned my gun on Los.

"Fool, you thought you killed her, but she survived!"

I said angrily as everybody else stepped out of the line of fire. They were totally surprised that I had my gun pointed at Los. Los, who put up his hands in shock, said;

"David what are you talking about. It wasn't me. You know I wouldn't do anything to her, especially at her place."

"I never said where I found her, so it was you."

My arm was stretched toward my one-time best friend, who was frightened because my gun was an extension of my arm as I pointed it at him. He pleaded for his life, but I wasn't hearing it. As I looked in his eyes, I felt my finger squeeze the trigger tighter and tighter before I heard a gun go off. I saw the bullets enter his flesh. When his body hit the ground, I heard his last breath as everyone around me laughed and celebrated. I was numb at the sight of the blood flowing freely from his lifeless body. Everything happened so fast, but there was only one thought on my mind...

Who fired the shots because I hadn't pulled the trigger? I looked around in terror knowing someone else did what I set out to do. It was at that moment I noticed the men had their weapons turned on me. Then one of them took my gun away. I heard laughter as a familiar figure emerged from the shadows. I stood motionless. His footsteps seemed abnormally loud as he walked closer to me. Isn't it funny how you can hear every little thing when you know you're at the end of your rope? Standing in front of me, he smirked and told me,

"You didn't see this coming, did you?"

The guy, who took my gun, gave it to him and he laughed as he pointed it at me.

27

It was Trey. I couldn't believe that he was here. I knew he wasn't dead, but still, it was like seeing a ghost. I had no idea he had been released. I was so consumed with getting out the game and being with Valencia that I was not prepared for his return. In light of the events surrounding him, I truly didn't expect to see him again. Trey smiled as he kicked Los' lifeless body and said,

"Well, it's about time you got what was coming to you."

He continued to speak to Los, like he could hear him,

"And let this be a lesson to ya!"

Trey kicked Los' body again, this time a bit harder. The fellas laughed boisterously. He looked at me and I tried to ease the mood by saying,

"When did you get out?"

"I was released last week. I knew nobody would be paying attention to me, especially since Ant was killed. But, I kept in contact with the men." He paused. "You see, David, they want to make money and everybody knew you wanted out. They knew it was only a matter of time before the operation was shut down and their money supply was cut. That's why they turned on you and now they will work for me. Tony and Don let me know you were coming here tonight and I thought to take this chance to get rid of you. Don't get upset, it's just the nature of the game, and you just got played."

I made a last ditch effort to calm the situation and save myself by saying,

"You know I had nothing to do with you going to jail or Ant being killed."

"You're right, I know it was all Los, but you, son, are a liability and I can't afford to have any loose ends."

I tell you, all the experiences I had up to this point does not compare to looking down the barrel of a gun knowing your number is up. All the money and fun I had was quickly forgotten as I awaited my death sentence at Trey's hands. But, for some reason Trey stopped and said,

"You know what, naw I'm not going to kill you yet. We are going to have some fun beating the daylights out of you and hearing you beg us to kill you."

Suddenly, I felt the hardest hit of my life as the punch landed in my face. I fell down next to Los' body as they kicked and stomped me. I was in so much pain I wanted them to shoot me to get this over with instead of enduring this pain, but I refused to beg. They kept up their deadly assault, and I felt pain in places on my body I never knew existed. Then they picked me up and threw me out of the window into the dumpster. I don't know if it was a blessing or a curse that the dumpster was open because of what I landed in. The stench was unlike anything I've ever smelled as it assaulted my stomach and gagged me. Finally, I heard Trey give them the order to shoot me as I lay in the dumpster.

"You should have stayed in church, but now it's your time to join Los in hell. Now, kill this fool."

I couldn't move because they'd beat me so bad. Even the sound of them cocking their guns did not give me any strength to move. Suddenly I heard sirens as the cops arrived on the scene. The fellas ran from the window. At that moment, somebody threw some bags over my face and closed the lid on me. I had to move my face so I could breathe. My whole body was covered, but I could still hear. I heard the cops say,

"Come out with you hands up!"

That is when all the shooting went on. I heard Trey saying Don and Tony was hit. It seemed like the gunfight went on for hours, until I heard something hard hit the top of the closed garbage can I was in. After that, it was silence. I heard the lid of the can being opened, but another cop said,

"There's no need to look in there, we got all of them. Let's get out of here."

So, the lid was dropped and silence fell except for the sound of cop cars leaving and sirens fading in the distance.

28

It's amazing how clear you can think when you believe you are near death. I lay in the dumpster broken and in pain. Time seemed to go very slowly as I laid there thinking about how different my life would have been had I stayed in the church like my mother wanted me too. I knew I definitely wouldn't be out here in a dumpster waiting to die. Tears ran down my face as I thought about how I would never see my dad, Valencia, Endia, and Keith again. I wished I could have just one more minute with them. It was so dark, I couldn't see a thing and then it hit me as to what my dad told me real fear was;

"And in hell he lift up his eyes, being in torments...." Luke 16:23

I knew this would be my fate as life left my body. I was going to knock the bottom out of hell. This would mean I would never see my mother again. I know to a lot of people, I'm not that bad of a person, but they are not the ones who set the standard, God is. Trey's last words to me really made me feel hopeless,

"You should have stayed in church, but now it's your time to join Los in hell."

I kept going in and out from the beating I took. I would see me and Valencia at our wedding. Then I would see our kids. I then saw images of my dad saying,

"He just said he was going to get his life right, but now he is in hell. Father give me strength."

Then I saw myself walk upon a casket with everyone crying in the background; Keith, Endia, Valencia, my dad, and even my godfather. I was wondering where was I, but I felt drawn to the casket and as I walked up and looked, it was me. It became so black, and then I saw a bright light. I heard,

"David. David. My poor boy, David."

I recognized the voice, could it be.

"Ma, is that you?" I said frightened.

"Yes, it's me." She said.

"Why can't I see you?" I asked feeling a sense of terror.

Sounding sad, my mother said,

"Because David, you are on your way to hell and light can't associate with darkness."

I felt a harrowing chill all over my body. I knew my time was up, and there was nothing I could do, but I had to try. I called out to her,

"Ma, please help me!" I yelled in desperation.

Sounding helpless, my mother said,

"I can't, but I told you who could. If he doesn't help you then we will be forever apart."

I woke up and at that moment, I remember my mother telling me if I ever found myself in a tough, situation to pray and God would help me.

My mother always said that God would help me as he did the Prodigal Son, but I had to call out to him. I kept hearing one verse the preacher used to say almost every Sunday,

"Train up a child in the way he should go: and when he is old, he will not depart from it." Proverbs 22:6.

Instantly, a lot of the verses and things my mother used to tell me about God came back to my remembrance. She always would tell me the story of the Prodigal Son,

"And he said, A certain man had two sons: And the younger of them said to his father, Father, give me the portion of goods that falleth to me. And he divided unto them his living. And not many days after the younger son gathered all together, and took his journey into a far country, and there wasted his substance with riotous living. And when he had spent all, there arose a mighty famine in that land; and he began to be in want. And he went and joined himself to a citizen of that country; and he sent him into his fields to feed swine. And he would fain have filled his belly with the husks that the swine did eat: and no man gave unto him. And when he came to himself, he said, How many hired servants of my father's have bread enough and to spare, and I perish with hunger! I will arise and go to my father, and will say unto him, Father, I have sinned against heaven, and before thee, And am no more worthy to be called thy son: make me as one of thy hired servants. And he arose, and came to his father. But when he was yet a great way off, his father saw him, and had compassion, and ran, and fell on his neck, and kissed him. And the son said unto him, Father, I have sinned against heaven, and in thy sight, and am no more worthy to be called thy son. But the father said to his servants, Bring forth the best robe, and put it on him; and put a ring on his hand, and shoes on his feet: And bring hither the fatted calf, and kill it; and let us eat, and be merry: For this my son was dead, and is alive again; he was lost, and is found. And they began to be merry..." Luke 15:11-24 "Now, if he was forgiven by his earthly father after asking for forgiveness, how much more would God forgive you." She always stressed.

I kept hearing her say,

"Pray David. God will hear you."

I prayed and prayed. I asked God to forgive me as the tears ran down my face. I said to God,

"If you give me another chance I will serve you from this day forth no matter what. I will marry Valencia and raise our children to fear and honor you, just like my mother tried to instill in me."

At that moment I heard,

"Young Blood are you still alive!?"

I groaned to let him know I was still alive. It was the bum that used to be a preacher. Somehow, he managed to get me out of the dumpster and carried me to the hospital.

29

When I arrived at the hospital, I was in and out of consciousness. The hospital staff needed my contact information so they went through my pockets and used my driver's license to contact my dad because I never changed my address. As I lay unconscious, I would hear muffled voices calling my name and speaking to me. I could only make out my dad and Endia's voices, although I heard other voices as well. I couldn't make out what they were saying, but I can say I was glad to hear them. There were many times I wanted to respond, but I couldn't. Eventually, I starting to make out Keith's and Valencia's voices, but still I could not talk back. This went on for what seems like forever, but one day all of a sudden I started to clearly hear my dad praying. I started groaning as I cracked my eyes. My dad called the nurses and doctor and they started checking my vitals and talking to me,

"David, can you hear me." Dr. Harris said.

I groaned.

"I'm going to take that as a yes. David, I want you to try to open your eyes."

I opened my eyes and then Dr. Harris had me go through another series of movements. It took a little while, but I was able to start talking after a few days. My dad told me what happened since that night,

"David, you were beaten pretty badly, almost near death. You had a few broken ribs and internal bleeding. You lost a lot of blood and needed a blood transfusion. Keith was your only blood match, so by the grace of God he was granted leave to provide the blood you needed for the transfusion." He paused. "You have been in and out of consciousness for about two months. Son, I was so worried about you, but God truly blessed and I am glad you are feeling better."

Hearing what my dad said made me think long and hard about the promise I made to God. I intended to keep the promise I made God because he spared my life. I knew if it wasn't for Him, I would not be alive. My thoughts were interrupted as my dad continued,

"Where do I begin, so much has happened? First, let me let you know that Valencia is doing fine. She came to see you about a month after you were admitted because she was pretty banged up herself."

That news made me happy, and I smiled as best I could as my dad continued,

"David, a few nights after you were admitted, I went to my car to get something I had left. When I came back, I noticed someone was in here with you and I heard them say;"

"I don't know if you can hear me. I just can't believe that this happened to you, you were getting out of the game. You were going straight." He paused as he shook his head. "I know that I was only able to talk to you slightly, but I want you to know that even though you are not my son, I loved you as my son." He paused. "Little Davie, you don't know this, but you were named after my son because your dad felt sorry for me because my son and my wife were killed when they shot up the drug house that night your dad took the bullet for me. I wanted to die with them, but I lived. I grew bitter, and became who I am today because I tried my best to not love anymore, so that I would not go through what I did when they were killed. Your dad quit the game because he saw how bad I had gotten after my wife and son died and he couldn't bear to think of that happening to you all. I let your dad know that I would never have children or get close to anyone like that again, so your dad named you after my dead son." He paused. "I'm so sorry that the lifestyle I chose kept me from you. I wanted so many times to come see you, do things for you, and just be there for you." Tears rolled down his face as he continued. "I would give anything to have you get better. Lord, you heard me! I will do anything to have my Little Davie better." My godfather said.

"Anything." My dad said as he walked in the room.

My godfather looked up at my dad and said,

"Leroy, you know what I mean. You know I've always loved Little Davie and I hate that my lifestyle has affected him like this."

"It wasn't your fault. He chose to do this." My dad paused. "Little Davie is in God's hands and I know the Lord will take care of him. David was pretty banged up, but the doctors say he is improving everyday and they expect him to make a full recovery."

My godfather sighed and said,

"That's good because I haven't been able to get any sleep since I heard what happened to him. Every time I tried to lie down, I would see images of him beaten, broken, and near death. Many times, I woke up with tears in my eyes. I know it was Little Davie that is going through this but then I kept thinking about my son. I just couldn't take it anymore, I had to see him, make sure he was ok." He paused. "Now, since I know he's ok. I got to go."

My dad stopped him and said,

"Now, I know you don't think I'm going to let you go that easy."

"What do you mean?" My godfather asked in surprise.

"Look, I am not going to allow you to dismiss God trying to talk to you. You are my brother and we always looked out for each other and I am not about to stop now."

My godfather sat down and listened to my dad.

"Patrick, you know that I was always willing to stick my neck out for you even if it meant my death. You were always like my little brother and I know that you got into this lifestyle following after me and for that I'm sorry. But, I want you to just hear me out." He paused. "You know when I was out there with you there was nothing I was afraid of until that day the house got shot up and Jacqueline and David was killed. I felt fear, thinking about what could happen to my wife and kids. So, I had to get out because I needed to, I lost my nerve." He continued. "Man, I am a Christian now and you know that I don't play games, I was always all in or all out when I was in something, so you know this is the real deal." He paused. "You don't know how long you got before your number is up. That is why you need to come on with me and give your life to Christ. You see I…"

My godfather interrupted my dad by saying,

"Man, I don't really want to hear this. That's cool for you, but not for me." My godfather said as he was getting up.

"Wait a minute. Let me finish, I took a bullet for you over some mess that you got us in, so I think I deserve at least 5 minutes of your time."

My godfather sat down.

"I'm trying to protect you from what's coming your way. All of us are going to die, but the question is; where are you going to spend eternity. We all know there's a God. No matter how much we try to deny it, God put that in us. I know you haven't been in a church since you were 11 and I was 13, but think about what you did when you thought David was dying, you prayed to God. You know that God is real." He paused walked over to my godfather and put his hand on his shoulder.

"Patrick, as your brother I must tell you that if you don't get right with God you are on your way to Hell and once you're there, there is no way out, ever." My dad looked at him intensely. "I had a preacher tell me a couple days ago that the Lord revealed to him that there was someone from my past that needed to be told about salvation because their days are numbered. I know he was speaking of you. He told me that if you didn't accept Christ on the day I talked to you, then there would be no more hope for you."

My godfather looked up, shook his head, and looked down at the floor and said,

"Why would God want me? I got my wife and son killed. I've murdered, sold drugs, and did all type of bad acts. So, why would God waste his time on me?"

"God loves you, that's why he wants you. God sent his Son Jesus, who died on the cross to pay for all of our sins; yours, mine, and everybody's. All you have to do is accept this gift by doing what God says in his Word."

"Then Peter said unto them, Repent, and be baptized every one of you in the name of Jesus Christ for the remission of sins, and ye shall receive the gift of the Holy Ghost." Acts 2:38.

My godfather sat for a minute, got up, put on his hat, and walked toward my dad and said,

"Leroy, I appreciate what you said, but this just isn't for me, I got to go."

As my godfather was leaving, my dad said,

"Patrick, I'll be praying for you. I hope the Lord shows mercy, before it's too late."

My dad shook his head as he continued to speak,

"A few days later, I heard that when your godfather left that night and went back to his place, he found out one of his men was plotting with a corrupt DEA agent to take him out and set himself up as the top guy. As far as anyone can tell they slit his throat, shot him in the head a few times, and dumped his body in a vacant lot." My dad said as tears rolled down his face.

I laid there in confusion as tears rolled down my eyes. I couldn't believe he was gone, taken out by his own men. I guess selling weed was not as safe as I thought. My dad continued,

"I warned him, but he just wouldn't listen and now there's no hope for him." He turned and looked at me and continued. "David this could be the only other chance you have to get right with God, so you better take it or no telling what might happen to you."

I thought long and hard about what my dad told me. All the things that happened in these last few months were crazy. Thinking back on that night everything went down, I found out that Trey was being followed by the cops in connection to Tina's murder, so they saw him enter the warehouse that night. Shortly after he entered, they heard him shoot Los. They went to their car and radioed for back up. Everything went down so quickly once the other cops arrived. They took down everybody in the warehouse. They never knew I was there because all they saw was a closed dumpster and didn't think anything of it. The last sound I heard was Trey's body hitting the dumpster after being shot and falling out the window. None of my blood was at the scene because I suffered internal injuries. They only found Trey's prints on my gun and the gun that killed Los. Since nobody survived, there was no way to tie me to the warehouse.

I couldn't stop thinking about that even though I didn't kill Los I felt an overwhelming sense of remorse because it was in my heart to kill him. Lying in my hospital bed thinking about what I was about to do to Los just tore me up inside. I realized how far my life had gotten out of control when I turned my back on God. Here I am laid up near death because I turned away from everything my mother taught me about serving God. I couldn't believe how far I had gotten away from the very essence of who I am to almost becoming a murderer and almost being murdered. I realized selling drugs and murder often go hand in hand in the game that's not a game at all. I recognized that God blessed me by not allowing me to kill Los. In my mind I knew I was blessed to not have pulled the trigger. Even though I thought, it would have been easy to live with killing Los after what he did to Valencia, looking at him pleading for his life made me hesitate in pulling the trigger. Killing him would have taken me to the point of no return because I would have had blood on my hands. For me, it would have been no turning back from the guilt that would have haunted me for the rest of my life. Yeah, he was wrong for what he did to Valencia, but still I can't just discount all the years we were friends. Each time I would have thought about something we did either as little kids or during this time, I would have remembered that I took his life and that would have been tough to live with. God knew that guilt, death, or prison would have been my life had I killed Los, even though I hadn't given it much thought. I could have ended up like Los, Ant, Trey, or my godfather, but God gave me a chance to have a life that didn't involve drugs, death, and prison and for that, I am grateful.

About the Author

Jerome D. Gibson MEd.

"It is my belief that reading should be exciting but not laced with all the profanity and lewd sex in most of the books today." says Award Winning Author Jerome D. Gibson.

"Many of our young people are reading, which is good, but what are they reading? When people used to say, "It doesn't matter what you read as long as you read", I know they had no idea what type of material would be available to our young people." Born and raised in Detroit Michigan, Jerome was educated in the Detroit Public School system. Jerome received his Bachelor of Science and Bachelor of Arts from Marygrove College, where he graduated with honors and completed a triple major in math, political science, and business Treyeting. He later received his teacher certification from Marygrove College. Jerome continued his education at Wayne State University, where he received his master's degree in math education.

Jerome has a deep concern for the material that young people are reading today. He was prompted to write this book after seeing what his students' were reading over the years that had no message and no life lesson in the material. It is ingrained in him to help students learn to develop higher order thinking skills, which most of the books they read lack. Also, this book has a spiritual message that reflects his deep belief in God and our Savior Jesus Christ. This message applies to adults as well as young people. Jerome is married and is an active member of Bethlehem Temple Church of Detroit.

Order Form

Calandra Publishing

P.O. Box 1296

Lincoln Park, MI 48146

(313) 355-7774

Name: _____

Address: _____

City/State: _____

Zip: _____

Email: _____

Title	Quantity	Total
More Than A Game-Book	___ x $15.00	$ _____
I'm Keeping My Money-Book	___ x $15.00	$ _____
Getting Out of Debt-CD	___ x $15.00	$ _____
I'm Keeping My Money-CD	___ x $15.00	$ _____
Total: **With Free Shipping and Handling**		$ _____

CPSIA information can be obtained at www.ICGtesting.com
226113LV00002B/109/P